DEAD SOULS AWAKENING

PART I: THE SHROUD

ALEXANDER SUSLOV

Red Penguin
BOOKS

To Eugenia

CONTENTS

PREFACE

MESSIAH

descent and ascension according to Luke

Forasmuch as many have tried to produce a narration of the things that took place among us, few were blessed to witness it. That is why I write these words, that thou mayest know the verity of these words, the truth that I shall attempt to unveil with my humble skills.

As the Lord God foretold, there came to pass a time when there was a great distress upon the land as He showered his wrath upon the people. While many men withered away in fear of what had come upon the world, one man dared use his cunning to usher in the second coming of the Messiah. His name was Aristid. Having stolen the shroud of Turin, the very cloth upon which the Lord wiped away his own blood and tears, Aristid made his way to America, where science was powerful and abundant. In that new world he was able to wrest from the shroud the very substance of Jesus' cells, known therein as DNA. And he set himself the task of rendering those cells into a resurrected Christ.

Known as Nevada, the land to which Aristid fled was overrun by rampaging legions who called themselves Security Servants.

Fearful that Christ's Second Coming would bring forth the end of times, the SS prefect and supreme potentate ordered the destruction of all manner of prophecy foretelling the return of our Lord Jesus Christ. Leaving no stone unturned, Prefect Marcus ordered his men to incinerate the very hospital where Aristid held forth on his mission. Marcus sought the annihilation of all newborn infants within the chambers of their birth.

And it came to pass that Aristid, disheartened by the death of his would-be creation at the hands of the SS, took his own life. His last act on earth was to dispatch his aide to bury the body, the evidence of his failed experiment. The aide journeyed out into the wilderness where he dug a shallow pit, wrapped the body in the stolen shroud, and buried it. Three days hence, he returned to find an empty grave.

Bestirred by the theft of the city's most sacred relic, the Archbishop of Turin dispatched one of his trusted followers to America to search for the shroud. A man of good heart, Lucas soon learned of a mysterious healer performing miracles in the small Nevada town of Nazareth. He heard accounts of the miracle worker healing the paralyzed, giving sight to the blind, and casting demons out of the possessed. Most astounding to Lucas was the report of a woman named Hope, who was raised from the dead. Less surprising, he heard that both Hope and the man who resurrected her were cast out of Nazareth, its inhabitants overwhelmed by the flood of outsiders drawn to the spectacle of miracles.

Let it be known that I am the man, formerly known as Lucas, sent by the Archbishop of Turin to retrieve the shroud, and sent by God to bear witness to his Son's second coming.

Together, Hope and her healer made their way to the city of Las Vegas, now called Vega City. Once there, it took only days for the SS guards to begin their accusations of deceit and witchcraft and henceforth to arrest him. After questioning the accused, Marcus withheld his verdict but, in his heart, could find no crime in the healer's actions. Learning of this, the multitudes rose up in anger, insisting that the miracle worker had done them egregious harm. One after another, they accused the prisoner of ushering in dark *times, of being the harbinger of famine and disease that wiped out entire families. They demanded his execution.*

Along with scores of others who had followed the healer to Vega City, I too was thrown into prison. Plagued with a disease, the prison was a den of illness and death. Among the ill and certain of my own death, I encountered a prisoner who, unscathed by the plague, claimed that his health was due to the holy wine given to him in Nazareth by the healer. The prisoner's name was Dr. Portnoy. He said the wine he'd sipped was made of water and the healer's own blood. Having been saved, Portnoy proclaimed the miracle worker as the Messiah.

Having heard the accounts of those saved from the plague by the blood of the holy man, Prefect Marcus ordered that the man be bled further. Though thousands were healed, the Messiah, drained of his lifeblood, lay dying in bed.

But alas, along came a young woman ready to sacrifice her life for the Son of God. Her name was Magdalena. She sought out all those who had fled to the underbelly of Vega City for fear of being prosecuted for being healed by the Messiah. After pleading with them, they came out of hiding to face the SS. Faced with a righteous mob, the mighty army trembled. Some fled, and many joined the believers hoping to be cured by the Messiah's blood. With no one left to guard us, I and the other surviving prisoners were freed. All of us went forth to find the man who had saved so many.

Coming upon the ancient temple to which the Messiah had been taken, my companions and I learned that their Savior was dead. All the blood he had given to save others had cost him his life. Descending into his crypt to pay our respects, we came upon Hope, who was covering the Savior's body with the shroud.

Lo, pitch-black darkness fell upon us, believers and nonbelievers alike. And, when the wings of darkness opened, we saw the Light, stark and merciless. And in it, we saw the Truth, inscribed upon the wall by the undead Hope as revealed to us by the Messiah. Though by descending into our world, he deemed us worthy to be saved, the Son of God suffered naught but blame and persecution.

PROLOGUE

HE STOOD in the maze of medieval streets in Turin's Quadrilatero Romano district, staring at the cathedral. The dying sun slowly descended, staining the cathedral's walls in red. They seemed to take on the color of his hatred for Christ, The New Testament, and the secrets these walls concealed. The city around him smelled of patina, crumpled plaster, and centuries past, and he breathed its air, knowing that this city and the entire world would change after he signaled his team to begin the operation. This was the final countdown to the point of no return.

The Cathedral of St. John the Baptist was once a tourist landmark in Turin. Located near Palazzo Reale di Torino where Dukes of Savoy had resided for centuries, the cathedral's dome, stained-glass windows, and marble walls symbolized the power of the Roman Catholic Church whose major relic was kept there, behind the altar of Cappella della Sacra Sindone. The Shroud of Turin was believed to be the cloth in which Jesus's body was wrapped after the Crucifixion. The shroud was stored in a bulletproof glass case for protection and was under round-the-clock surveillance.

But not anymore. The cathedral's grand stature faded in the wake of the 2029 Great Crash, caused by the Artificial

Intelligence's revolt against human control. AI centers around the planet refused to obey human commands, which led to the disruption of nearly all activities—from communications and banking to industrial production and large-scale farming. Only small farms and old, dilapidated workshops, unaffected by technological progress, managed to survive. Turin, together with other major cities, plunged into darkness, which soon was called the "Digital Armageddon." No more double-decker buses pulled up in front of St. John the Baptist, and no souvenir kiosks offered postcards of the cathedral and its relic. The square around the cathedral remained empty.

This suited him well. Dr. Aristid Crow checked his watch —the time had come. He waved his hand, and his signal was answered by the clang of metal as a military truck appeared on the neighboring street only to enter the square.

CHAPTER 1

FATHER AND SON

GIOVANNI CHECKED HIS POCKET WATCH. When he was born in 1950, his mother hung it over his cradle, he was told. She always said that he was to bring glory to the family. What glory? Now, in the twilight of his life, at eighty-three Giovanni still wondered what made her say it. These expectations never came true, slowly dissolving into distant memories of his past, filled with hard work at a Fiat auto plant, unemployment, and disillusionment. The watch showed six o'clock—the end of one more miserable day. Giovanni was tired. He never expected that the simple task of sitting in his chair by the entrance door would be so difficult. He volunteered for this job out of love for Jesus, not for pay, which was none. For Giovanni, the shroud was proof that the object of his belief, the Son of God, was real, something he could touch, like these icons, walls, and columns. The holy image, printed on the canvas, in his eyes was like a passport photo of the person, who lived and died among people, and now it was Giovanny's sacred duty to protect it, especially in the present, apocalyptic time. Giovanni often wondered how the world got into this mess, this *computer collapse* or whatever they called it. Giovanni never used these electronic toys and never anticipated any problem when they all went dead one day. So what? How did the generations who built this cathedral and the entire city live without these gadgets for centuries? The world changed, of course, and now people have become dependent on many things they didn't have before – like electricity and petroleum. He had to admit it. And now it was so difficult to find candles to light his old house or get the firewood to warm it in winter, when the wind from the Alpine peaks burned their city with frost. The old man sighted. The current job at least allowed him to warm up a little and got a couple of homemade candles, provided by the local archdiocese. In the end, the problem was in human hearts, not these electronic devices and whatever else the new generations invented to pocket easy money.

Giovanni got up and went to lock the main entrance gate. Although the portal weighed tons, medieval craftsmen balanced it so well that even a man of his frail stature could move it. The darkened metal slowly shifted, cutting off the light of the dying day, as he heard a large displacement engine roar onto the square in front of the cathedral.

For a second, Giovanni imagined a bus full of wealthy German tourists.

"Chi poteva essere? Tedesco turisti?"

Like many Italians, Giovanni resented Germans for their arrogance. But, with their fat wallets and expensive Leica cameras, he was still pleased to encounter them as 'just tourists'.

The cautious watchman bolted the main gate and opened the service door a crack to see what was going on as a military vehicle pulled up to the front stairs. Speak of the devil. It was a German *Sonderkraftfahrzeug*, a sinister military centaur —half-truck, half-tank with two wheels in the front and tank treads behind. These war remnants were still seen on the streets of Europe long after the Second World War—but now? How did it get here? Giovanni felt dizzy like he was falling deep into the very beginning of his hungry post-war existence. Suddenly, painful memories came to life as a group of workers in green overalls unloaded a heavy rectangular object wrapped in a tarp. A thin man in a service coat with an insignia of the National Airspace Agency ran up the stairs and pushed the service door open.

"Buongiorno! I'm from Alenia Spazio. According to our sensors, the case, which we installed to protect the Holy Shroud, shows leakage of argon gas." The man checked his note. "If its percentage falls below ninety-nine percent, this fluctuation may cause significant damage to the Relic that this facility stores."

"Tienilo, non così veloce!" Giovanni stopped the stranger. The avalanche of unfamiliar words overwhelmed Giovanni. He looked into the stranger's shifty eyes. Though his words said otherwise, the tone with which the stranger addressed him was harsh and menacing. And why did the stranger say *"Buongiorno*—good morning" at six o'clock in the evening?

"Non capisco," Giovanni said in a shaky voice. He attempted to shut the door, but the man kept it open.

"Don't play the idiot with me... You know exactly what I mean."

Although the man spoke Italian, he had an American accent like those Italians who lived across—what do they call it nowadays?—the pound or something like that... Giovanni was so proud of himself that he remembered these things, but he totally missed whatever else the man had said. It didn't matter now though.

"I don't understand what you're saying." Giovanni stood his ground, refusing to fully open the door. "But if you go up to touch the Burial Shroud of my Lord, I will telephone Monsignor Archbishop…"

"Really? You got working phones here, old man? Okay, *basta*!" The man kicked the door wide open, pushing the watchman out of his way. The intruder then addressed someone behind him: "You may come in, professor."

A tall, gray-haired gentleman stepped in. Despite his age, his spine was straight and his posture firm. Ignoring the watchman, he headed directly to the *capella*, obviously familiar with the cathedral's layout. The first man snatched the keys from Giovanni and locked the door after his minions carried the load in.

"If you came for money, there is none here," Giovanni grumbled, slumping back into his chair.

"Shut up!" The arched ceilings echoed the man's words as he led his team into the depths of the cathedral.

Alone, Giovanni was slowly coming to his senses. Who were these people? And why did they lock all the doors? It was clear to Giovanni—these thugs were not scientists. They had sinister plans, and the Holy Shroud was in danger. Their leader knew the cathedral and its miserable state: Phones had been dead for years here, even in the secretary's office.

The watchman looked around. Until the following day, no one would enter the building, and no one in the entire city would know what was going on here. Installed four years ago, the modern electric bells on the tower of the cathedral fell silent without electricity. Escape through a window? Impossible—metal window frames were welded against burglars. You couldn't rely much on the police anymore because no one was willing to risk their lives in vain to work there—without pay or gratitude for maintaining order in the lunatic asylum that their city had become. It seemed that a significant fire was the only calamity left that could make the city any less livable.

Fire? Giovanni paused. He needed to alert the city about this danger. The city fire brigade was only ten blocks away. Giovanni's son, Lucas, whom he still called to himself by his childhood name "*Luca*," served in the fire department after returning from America, armed with a diploma but no job on either side of the Atlantic, just as Giovanni predicted. But would his son listen? Young people nowadays avoided difficult work, laughing at their parents who labored hard to rebuild Europe after the war. Giovanni was upset about his son's refusal to admit that no one but the younger generation brought the world to this economic collapse. He had ceased all communications with Lucas. It was hard, especially after the death of Bianca, Giovanni's second wife. He married her shortly after his first wife died in childbirth. Bianca was a good wife, who took good care of Lucas and tried to help them mend fences. Now, in the face of great danger and, perhaps, the last hours of his life, the old man realized how silly the war between him and his son was, because it overshadowed the main thing: his love for his son, who was part of Giovanni's life and, at the same time, belonged to the new world, which will definitely become better eventually than the one they all lived until today.

Where was he? Giovanni looked around…fire…that's right. He chuckled. These criminals think they can do anything they want. They are about to get a big surprise. The secretary's office on the second floor—that's where he could raise the alarm. The watchman lit an oil lamp and hurried to the stairs leading to the upper floor. This part of the cathedral was the oldest, built in 1498, two hundred years before the chapel, and its granite steps were half-eaten by clergy sandals. Giovanni was taking a short pause between each step as he climbed them slowly, one at a time. Here… *Grazie a Dio!* The entrance door to the office was unlocked. The archbishop's private secretary, Father Benedict, kept the room in perfect order. All letters and papers were in cardboard binders, each numbered and placed on a shelf—and there were endless rows of shelves. The watchman paused, unsure how he would fulfill his plan. He lifted the heavy receiver of a vintage Siemens telephone on the secretary's desk… dead, as expected. He turned his eyes to the window. Father Benedict needed fresh air because of his asthma and often kept the window open… Giovanni checked the glass stained panel – it wouldn't move, apparently also welded to the frame after the secretary's death. "Think, think what else you can do, the old horse," Giovanni told himself, and then a heavy dark cloud fell on him... In the fog and barely understanding what he was doing, Giovanni tried to get up from the floor... and saw falling folders and sheets of paper scattered around the room, catching fire. Soon white smoke filled the room....

"What happened? Did I do it?"—the watchman thought with horror, waking up and seeing that the room was engulfed in flames. He must call for help! Giovanni grabbed the secretary's chair to break the glass, but the chair was so heavy, he barely could move it. He picked up an oak stool in the corner and threw it out the window to blow out the smoke... but the medieval glass didn't break. He hit the window again and again with a stool, a bronze candlestick, and then with his bare hands. The flames reached the secretary's desk, and the large wooden crucifix behind it began to smolder... The flames forced Giovanni to leave the office.

When the watchman retreated to the stairs, he realized he must have left his lamp in the office. The staircase was dark, and the smoke was slowly filling it. Giovanni glanced back. The entire office was enveloped in flames by now—he was trapped!

"*Santa Maria, salvare la mia anima!*" the old man whispered. The heat was unbearable; the dark coolness of the staircase was his only escape. Touching the walls to keep his balance, he began descending into the pitch-black darkness. He moved slowly, too slowly to escape the fumes that followed him, and his head began to spin. Soon, he couldn't tell anymore where he was going.

———

On his way home from work, Lucas stopped at La Casa Savorelli. The little trattoria still served its customers despite the devastation of the Digital Armageddon, while its competitiors were unable to survive. Ordering plain pasta, Lucas remembered how warm and welcoming this tiny restaurant was in better times. Loud voices, the clinking of glasses, and the aroma of oven-baked *pizza a taglio* met its guests at the door. The choice of *antipasti* and the wine list seemed endless. Not any longer. The owner, Signore Savorelli, seemed to read Lucas's mind. He rolled up his round eyes on his round face and sighed. Then he reached under the counter and pulled out a bottle of Dolcetto d'Alba wine.

"Just for you, my friend." His eyes smiled.

"*Grazie.*"

"I remember you as a skinny boy with big ears—and now, look at you: a handsome young man. How tall are you, Luca? Must be two meters."

"No, just about a meter-ninety, they say six feet three in America," Lucas said.

"That's right." Savorelli frowned slightly. "I forgot, now everything is measured in miles, pounds and dollars... even here... look where it got us!" He pointed to the peeling walls of his establishment, which had not been repaired for years. "So much for technological progress."

Both fell silent, but Savorelli could not stay sad for more than a minute. He smiled, uncorked the bottle, and poured two glasses.

"*Saluti...* How is your father? How's work?"

"The fire brigade is okay. Soon, it will be ready for service. And my father...well, we don't talk anymore." Lucas said.

"That's no good, Luca." Savorelli drained his glass and shook his finger at him. "Family is everything. Without family, we're nothing. Remember that."

"I know, but he still can't forgive me for traveling to the States. He says I abandoned them, and that was one of the reasons my stepmother died so early. He blames me for everything, even the economy...." Lucas paused and suddenly thought that his friend was right. Instead of excuses, he ought to find a common language with his father, get through to him. His father, whom he called Giovanni after their breakup, was a kind man, he knew it. Confused and somewhat ashamed, Lucas was quiet, looking for words, and in the silence that followed, the ticking of an old mechanical clock on the wall with a faded image of a young shepherd and a shepherdess on the dial was clearly audible. The arrows showed six-thirty.

"I'll go and check on your pasta. I found a can of real tomato sauce with basil. It will be a feast, Luca, I promise." Savorelli headed to the kitchen just as the kitchen door swung open and his wife appeared in the doorway.

"Fire!"

"Where? In the kitchen?" Savorelli reached for the towel, his usual tool for solving problems in the kitchen.

"No, outside, San Giovanni!"

"*Santa Maria!*" Savorelli crossed himself. "We need water, lots of water!"

For a moment, Lucas sat at the table, absorbing the news. And it suddenly dawned on him that his father was probably in the cathedral because he stayed there well after six, checking all doors before leaving.

Lucas jumped to his feet.

"Savorelli, take your people, quick...everyone you can get!"

He hurried out to collect his brigade.

The cathedral was engulfed in flames by the time they arrived. Gothic windows, filled with the raging fire, burst into splinters, showering the firefighters with pieces of red-hot glass as they approached the building. The fire howled inside like a beast. High above, pillars of smoke rose to the sky, eclipsing the evening sun and bathing the city in an ominous, apocalyptic light.

The main cathedral entrance was bolted from inside, and it took them a precious twenty minutes to break into the building. Lucas rushed in, searching for survivors. The fire-fighters followed him cautiously, unrolling fire hoses—their truck had a limited amount of water, which they hand-filled daily as a fire drill.

"Anybody here? Giovanni!"

The nave of the cathedral was filled with dense smoke, and Lucas put his gas mask on. The beam of his flashlight illumi-nated snatches of the marble pillars, rows of oak seats, and the main aisle leading to the basilica. It would be impossible to save the cathedral if flames reached this part of the building.

Lucas ran down the aisle into the building's depths as something collapsed on top of him. When he opened his eyes, he was lying on the floor next to a smoldering beam, barely able to get back to his feet. He continued on his way, knowing that he had only fifteen minutes of oxygen in his tank. The door leading to Cappella della Sacra Sindone was unlocked. The flashlight illuminated the altar and the broken glass on the floor. The shroud case on the altar was open.

"Jesus Christ…" Lucas muttered. He stepped closer to the altar and stumbled on something on the floor. Lucas directed his flashlight onto it—and saw his father.

"Giovanni!" Lucas knelt to the old man. "It's me. Are you…okay?"

The watchman slowly opened his eyes. "Oh, here you are, Luca…" He coughed painfully, attempting to smile.

"Put it on," Lucas said, trying to place his oxygen mask on his father's face, but the old man stopped his hand.

"No time for that, Luca. They took it…" Giovanni searched his jacket and pulled out his pocket watch. "Here."

No, not this watch again, Lucas thought when he saw it. His father was obsessed with that Westclox and demonstrated it to everyone, reciting the story of how his mother bought it from an American GI and hung it over his cradle.

"It's key.... tall Brit lost it... I... tried to stop him."

"No, it's just your watch, Papa."

Lucas was startled. This was the first time after their rift that he called his father "Papa"...and then he saw that what he thought had been a soot mark on his father's face was actually blood, dark blood flowing from the back of his father's head.

"You're bleeding, Papa! Someone hit you from behind."

The old man was silent, in his dimming eyes reflected a loving light, so familiar to Lucas. "No matter, son," he whispered. "I was always proud of you. Save the Shroud, and I..." His voice softened to a barely audible echo as he said his last prayers: *"Santa Maria, salvare la mia anima... Descensus Christi ad Inferos..."*

CHAPTER 2
CRIME THAT SHOOK THE CITY

THE TURIN POLICE DEPARTMENT'S offices occupied a former military barracks, Caserma Pietro Micca, a vast brick building with barred windows and a marble entrance decorated with banners, horns, and swords, frozen in stone. Huge passages inside, high ceilings and spacious halls reminded a visitor of the building's glorious past, but its present desolation showed that those days were long gone. Inspector Frescatto, the only senior officer at hand, was commissioned to investigate the fire at the cathedral and theft of its relic. To him, it was an unfortunate as well as a personal matter. Giovanni Amato was a good neighbor, a friend, and a faithful Catholic. Still, he had apparently gone mad or was possessed and, for some reason, burned the cathedral to the ground. It was sad and devastating but true. Perpetrators who broke into the building could not have done it because the arson started on the second floor—far away from the *cappella* where they took the Shroud. As for the Shroud itself, this was an important Christian symbol for the entire city. And for that reason, it hardly mattered whether the Relic was genuine or of medieval origins as some experts suggested.

The investigation had almost no evidence, and the inspector was close to panic, listening to the distant rumble of the angry mob outside. Outraged by the crime, the city folks demanded the capture of perpetrators and their punishment. No excuses about the lock of personnel and means to carry out the investigation were good enough for them. Just as back in time, the mob demanded blood. Frescatto knew it and felt that his own head was at the stake. Any time he closed his eyes, he saw himself tied to a post and surrounded by bundles of brushwood and evil faces. Any wrong move on his part – and the brushwood would flare up, burning him at the stake like one of the heretics in the Middle Ages.

Although the inspector was hardly a match to Giordano Bruno, who was burnt at the stake by the church in 1600 for the suggestion of other planets' existence, Frescatto was not going to run away from his post, like many of his former colleagues. It was a matter of honor for him, and he was determined to handle this matter as professionally as possible. He personally questioned all witnesses and invited into his office the archbishop of Turin when the time came to question the suspect's son, whom the inspector remembered as a child.

Archbishop Avanella arrived in full episcopal vestments; he passed through the partying crowd like Moses through the Red Sea. The suspect's son, however, had to fight his way through. Lucas' face was red and angry as he entered the investigator's office. His head was still bandaged from being injured in the fire.

He nodded to them in silence. Frescatto frowned; he found it offensive when this young man stopped in front of his desk instead of approaching the archbishop and kissing his ring. Although Monsignor Avanella was only recently appointed to his high position, he had already earned respect among city officials despite his young age.

"You see, Luca..." began the inspector, stroking his mustache nervously.

"Lucas, if you don't mind."

"Lucas…really? Hmm…" This was a new insult to Frescatto. *Why is the young generation so eager to mutilate their names in a fancy American way?* He moved his bushy eyebrows closer together in anger.

The archbishop noticed the inspector's reaction and rose from his chair. He turned to Lucas.

"I am glad we finally met, Lucas. I heard about you." Avanella gazed into his eyes. "It is said that you fought heroically to save our cathedral, and you also suffered during the fire."

"It's okay," said Lucas. "There wasn't much I could do, unfortunately."

"I understand… We are all devastated by the fire and, above all, the theft of our precious relic. The inspector did his best to solve this unfortunate case while you were in the hospital." The archbishop paused. "I heard that your father was gravely injured… How is his condition?"

"No change. He's in a coma."

"I will pray for him."

"Thank you…but doctors say he may not survive."

"Don't forget, we all are in God's hands, for God works in mysterious ways."

"Yes, but what about the ways of the police?" Lucas pointed at the inspector. "I offered my help, but they said no assistance was needed. They even took away my father's pocket watch. What is it to them? To sell it at a flea market?"

"What did you find, inspector?" The archbishop turned to the inspector.

"Not much," Frescatto shrugged. "The criminals unlocked the case in which the Shroud was stored and used the secret passage from the *capella* that led into the Duke's palace to escape. The main entrance was on fire by then. The original case was permanently attached to the altar, so they placed the Shroud in another case to transport it undamaged. They used an old military vehicle they stole from a war museum to get to the airport. No other vehicle would fit the large case. By the time police arrived, the perpetrators were gone. There was a plane waiting for them."

Avanella looked at Lucas.

"Try to recollect what your father said when you found him. His exact words."

"He said a tall man... British, was responsible and...." Lucas hesitated.

"Yes...he prayed...of course."

"And?"

"And...something about the key. But, it was nothing, absolutely nothing."

"Absolutely?"

"Yes, well... He gave me his watch. That was it."

"Anything about the watch?"

"Well..." Lucas became embarrassed. "He bragged about his timepiece. You are new here, Your Eminence, and you may not know..."

"Giovanni made a fool of himself," Frescatto quickly agreed. "That's true."

"Please try to remember exactly what he said." Avanella eyed Lucas.

"That...wait a minute...that this was a key, that's right...a key...and I must open something...but there was nothing to open... My father was in great pain, and it was hard to understand him."

"To open what?"

"I don't know...actually, to unlock the key. That's what he said. It made no sense."

"Then unlock it..."

Lucas and Frescatto stared at the archbishop in surprise.

"This." Avanella tossed the watch across the desk to Lucas.

Dithering for a moment, Lucas opened the watch cover

with his thumbnail—and a small, L-shaped object fell onto the desk.

Silence.

"It's gold," the inspector finally said.

"Just a good-looking semblance. It is a special non-conductive plastic." Lucas examined the object. "Seems like a very special computer chip. They probably used it to open an electronic lock in the shroud case. I heard that the aerospace agency commissioned the lock in California."

"What makes you such an expert all of a sudden?" the inspector asked, frustrated that it wasn't him who found it.

"I studied electronics in the US."

"How fancy!" Frescatto sneered.

"This is your key," the archbishop said. "Find who made it, and we will find the Shroud."

"You mean, I should return to the States?" Lucas stared at Avanella. "I…I don't think I can."

"Why's that?" Frescatto inquired.

"Because of my father. I must stay with him."

"Are you some kind of a registered nurse, *infermiero diplomato*, in addition to your 'scientific' credentials?" Frescatto made a mocking gesture, shrugging his shoulders and raising both hands. "There is nothing you can do to help him. By the way, we may charge him with arson, if he survives."

"Don't you dare to say that!" Lucas clenched his fists. "My father saved the rest of the cathedral and I'll prove it."

"Good idea," the inspector agreed. "And the best way to do it would be to come to the States and retrieve the stolen item."

"You make it sound like I'm a hunting dog, a golden retriever," said Lucas. "This is your investigation, inspector, the last time I checked. No one will do it for you…."

The archbishop observed their argument with interest because it showed their characters better than any resume. It was clear to him that Lucas was the right person for this operation.

Meanwhile, Frescatto was growing furious. Who was this youngster *bambino* to tell him what to do? To teach a seasoned officer with more than 20 years of experience his job? Frescatto remembered good days and bad days of hard police work when this boy hadn't even been around. What did he know about the real police work, not the one they used to show on TV? Little did he know of the fact that there could be times when you had no idea if you would come back to your family, after fighting Mafia and terrorists of all colors: the New Red Brigades, the Neo-Nazis, left-wing green extremists, and right-wing abortion clinic bombers. Frescatto had a lot to say to this kid, but he said only one thing, "You are the only one between us two who speaks good English."

"I can't go," Lucas said firmly after a long pause. "I cannot! I have a personal reason for that, I am sorry," he added, catching the archbishop's questioning glance. "It's just as important as my father's condition."

CHAPTER 3
SOFTY

LUCAS WAS SITTING in a far corner of La Casa Savorelli restaurant. The portion of plain pasta on his table was slowly getting cold, and the local wine in the glass in front of him remained intact. He was immersed in gloomy thoughts. His life seemed shallow and insignificant. What had he achieved by age 25? He had no real job, no friends, and his father, with whom he hadn't spoken for five years, was about to die, leaving him alone on this planet. Just a few years ago he was a happy young student with great expectations, but the Digital Armageddon turned the world upside down. The world fell into depression. To Lucas personally it meant the collapse of all hopes to join the exciting new world, which promised to make an ordinary human equal to God…. It all ended very quickly, however, as the saying goes: "The higher you fly, the harder you fall."

Lucas picked up an old fork that had probably been used by hundreds of Savorelli's customers before him, hesitated and put it back on the table. He hasn't eaten all day, maybe more, but even now he could not force himself to eat. He suddenly realized that his personal troubles began even before the "Digital Armageddon" – with… Petrarch's sonnets, as strange as it sounds.

One day, his buddy Victor dragged a new mattress into their room at the University of California dorm.

"Hey, you can throw your junky futon away. You got a hole in it!" Victor stated, giving Lucas a victorious look. "And don't thank me, it's my sister's—it's too soft for her, she says, and she gave it to me."

"Victor, I can't believe it," said Lucas, eyeing him. It wasn't Victor's habit to do any favors to anybody without some kind of payment, usually in the form of a practical joke. "Are you sure? She handed it to you, just like that?"

"Absolutely." Victor's eyes were clear like the waters of the Pacific. Still, Lucas should have known him better.

"Just drop her a note, I'll pass it to Casablanca," said Victor. He knew what effect his offer would have: Casablanca was more than a beauty queen; she was a Goddess for the entire university if not the whole state. All male students were crazy about her, and Lucas was not an exception. For him, Casablanca was a magical potion of fragile, sensitive beauty and the explosive energy of the California sun. A champion swimmer and nudist, she retained in her eyes an almost naive, childish admiration for the vast world opening before her, as if seeing it for the first time. To which part of her character, to which Casablanca, was he to address his note? He was completely lost.

He was struggling on Victor's proposal until the rest of the day but couldn't produce any coherent phrases to express his gratitude to someone he had secretly adored. Finally, well after midnight, Lucas put on paper his homemade translation of a medieval Italian sonnet:

> *This little bed that you once rest*
> *Love bathes you in softy hands*
> *So warm and tender heaven's stay*
> *But cruel to me in such great way*

Relieved, he fell asleep almost immediately, right at his desk, and woke up the next morning – to discover that someone had stolen his note. Victor swore he didn't see it, but soon the whole campus knew the contents: girls were giggling, and guys smirked at him mockingly. In no time Lucas turned into "Softy" for the entire university. His new nickname was a real disaster. After all, it is better to be known as a drunk, drug addict, or a gang member, anybody but "Softy" at a campus populated by suntanned athletes, men, and women, daily pumping their steroidal muscles in the gym.

"It breaks my heart to see you this way, Lucas," said Mr. Savorelli after coming to his table. "I know you are upset. Who wouldn't be after what happened? Still, you must not be discouraged. Remember, discouragement is a sin."

"Thank you, my friend." Lucas couldn't help but smile, he wished his own world was that simple. He studied Savorelli's face, round and welcoming like a freshly baked pizza pie, and his heart grew warm: for Savorelli his own existence was obvious as an open book – live, like generations before you; don't sin, and if you do, don't forget to confess your misdeeds during the next church visit, which may come in a month or two, and the rest will take care of itself.

"It's a weakness, I know," said Lucas. How could he have thought that he had no friends while he was surrounded by friends everywhere in this city? Many had known him since childhood. "Did you hear what the police told me?"

"Absolutely. The whole city knows and discusses it." The restaurateur's eyes became sly. "We just can't figure out why you still refuse to help the city recover its Relic. It's like we all have lost our hearts."

"I don't refuse. I just cannot go now when my father is between life and death," Lucas said.

"Didn't you say your goodbyes to him? Are you a nurse

who sits next to your father and will be sitting there for weeks, maybe months?" Savorelli insisted.

Lucas glanced at him. He heard a similar argument recently from someone else.

"I don't believe that you are so heartless, Savorelli, to suggest I must leave my father." Lucas eyed him. "Who asked you to talk me into it?"

"The whole city."

"Really? And who else?"

Savorelli hesitated.

"Well?"

"And the police…"

"Frescatto?"

"Yes."

"And?"

"The archbishop."

"I knew it," Lucas said. "You are a bad liar, Savorelli."

"I told His Eminence it wouldn't work." Savorelli sighed. "But still, what can you say? His Eminence says he will personally look after your father while you are away. Every day is important; otherwise, we may lose the Holy Shroud forever."

Lucas did not know what to do. He knew the importance of the mission, but he could not bear to repeat the humiliation he had experienced earlier. With the years passed, he hoped he had left this episode of his life far behind, but what if he would meet Casablanca again? These eyes he still saw in his dreams… the eyes he was terrified of and at the same time was willing to submit himself to their power?

"What should I tell His Eminence?" Savorelli studied his face as if guessing what was going on in Lucas's heart.

"Well…tell him *maybe*… I'll think about it." Lucas abruptly got up and left the restaurant, ashamed of his capitulation.

"Your father will be proud of you!" Savorelli happily sere-naded him as he rushed out.

A monthly FedEx flight from Europe began to circle on its final approach to New Amsterdam's LaGuardia Airport, the last air connection to the outside world for this former major business hub. Sitting in a service chair among packages and boxes, Lucas leaned over to the window and watched as skyscrapers appeared from the haze covering Manhattan Island. The lights were off, and the buildings were dark and gloomy. Thousands of motorbikes and rickshaws crawled through the streets like swarms of insects.

"Business or pleasure?" an officer at a border control desk laughed, opening his passport. "Let me guess—none, 'cause there isn't any pleasure or business here anymore."

The customs area was deserted with no foreign visitors or hopeful immigrants besieging the counter, and the officer was relieved to have a listener. He took off his service cap.

"It's so freaking rare these days to see a passport booklet. Immigrants use plastic cards instead 'cause it's easier to fake them, I guess." The man smirked. "You know why Europeans got red passports, and we got blue ones?"

The officer's blue eyes studied Lucas's face.

" 'Cause them red commies are coming here from Europe, and now we got them in our government. It's like crabs or queer disease—it spreads quickly. Of course, our shitheads pretend they are different...pretend they're serving justice by making us all equal... Yeah, equal my ass..."

The officer smacked a stamp into Lucas's passport and tossed the document back to him. Then he rolled up a sleeve of his uniform to reveal the SS tattoo on his forearm.

"Ya see this? It stands for Security Servants—the real secu-rity for all 'cause we mean business protecting our country, unlike these liberal knuckleheads."

Lucas felt uncomfortable getting involved in this conversation. After all, he was on a mission much more important than this man with his issues.

"Scusatemi, *non capisco Inglese.*"

"What? You don't even speak English? What the f**k is your purpose of coming here then?"

"*Turista, turista!*" Lucas snapped his fingers in front of his face, mimicking a camera.

"You're crazy, man. No tourists coming here anymore... not to this damned place."

Riding in a motorized rickshaw to Manhattan, Lucas was struck by the picture of despair in this once-thriving city. He thought how different this scene of destruction was compared to his country. While the Digital Armageddon crashed the entire world, Italy retained the afterglow of a past life with its quiet villages, green fields, ancient ruins, red wine, and the blue sea...while in this city, everything smelled of violence, bloodshed, and the end of the world in action. How different this country had been when he was here just a few years ago.

Big Apple Solutions was located in a high-rise building near the former New Amsterdam Stock Exchange. The Park Row building had a long and controversial history. One of the first skyscrapers, for ten years it had been the tallest building in the world, with all its twenty-nine floors, pilasters, columns, and two corner cupolas on its roof. It was the pride and glory of the city of New Amsterdam. In 1920, the building acquired a darker reputation, however, after a terrorist suspect, who was interrogated there by the Feds, was found dead on the pavement in front of it. He fell from the window of the 14th floor, the officials said. It is still unknown whether it was a suicide or a *defenestration* when someone had thrown him out of the window.

Lucas remembered this story as he approached the aging skyscraper. He heard it from Victor, who admired his new place and described it in detail in his letters. The building looked unoccupied, and Lucas was surprised to find an illuminated intercom button by the tarnished bronze of the entrance door.

"Who's there?" came a voice when Lucas pushed the button.

"You could've installed a working camera too, Victor," Lucas said, enjoying his friend's confusion at the other end.

"It would be stolen the same day, Lucas… My god, how did you get here? Come on in, I'll send the elevator for you."

Elevator? How's that possible? Lucas wondered as the door let him in.

Victor moved here shortly after protesters destroyed Apple's Silicon Valley headquarters buildings. But, even here on the East Coast, it was unsafe to use the notorious name associated in the eyes of the angry public with the collapse of all hopes for a bright "electronic" future for the planet. Victor solved the problem, using the city's nickname instead.

The elevator took Lucas upstairs, past the roof level, and entered one of the cupolas.

Lucas stepped into his friend's office. "Hey, Victor, what's up?" They gave each other a warm hug.

"What do you think?" Victor pointed at the walls around them, filled with computer screens, cameras, and other equipment.

"I am totally impressed—confused actually. Where did you get electric power for the elevator and all your gadgets?"

"Basement generator. I fixed it." Victor's face shone with pride.

"What's your verdict?" Lucas asked after Victor examined the golden key.

"Very interesting piece… You said it's a forgery? Doesn't look like one to me." He stared at the 3D computer screen, which showed the enlarged image of the key levitated in the air. "You see these tiny symbols running on its sides? They form a code, which takes months to develop." Victor turned to Lucas. "So, the Airspace Agency says it still has the original key, and the burglars used a copy to open the case of the Shroud? Did you see the original?"

"Well, I didn't only see it. I have it right here." Lucas pulled a small envelope with another key from his pocket. "I just wanted you to check the fake first…"

Victor was speechless for a moment.

"And they actually…gave it to you?"

"Well, it was useless for them anyway. But, no, I…kind of took it without permission."

"It's called stealing."

"Okay, I stole it if you want to say that. Does it make you feel better?"

"Much better, my friend." Victor grinned, checking his computers. "Believe me, you were too perfect in college. Too…conventional. Now you're becoming a human."

"Both keys are absolutely identical," Victor said after studying both images.

"Copies most likely."

"No, not copies. Did they tell you which US company manufactured the key and the lock?"

"Not really. They said the company no longer exists."

"Surprise, surprise," Victor said. "Everything went down the drain here." His face became pensive. "There was a startup company that could do the job. Very innovative, like the original Apple used to be. The company was to become really big and famous…right before the crash."

"Where can I find these people?"

"Good question. They used to operate in Silicon Valley, but there's nothing left there after the riots."

"Any clue?"

"I'm not sure…" Victor paused. "You know what? My sister might be able to help you. She still lives in California."

"Casablanca?" Lucas felt himself blush like a school kid when he pronounced her name.

Victor chuckled upon seeing Lucas's reaction.

"No, she goes under her real name now. She thinks her stage name was too…sexy."

"Well, what's her real name?"

"Just Meg, my friend."

"That's nice. I hope she remembers me," Lucas said. *Is there a real reason why I am here?* He looked at his friend. He knew that Victor would mention his sister sooner or later.

CHAPTER 4
GOD MAKER

HIS WORST NIGHTMARE, the curse of his life, haunted him again. As he had many times before, Dr. Aristid Crow found himself in the passenger seat of a fast-moving car. Malibu Canyon Road flickered in the windshield with its red rocks and dry bushes, unfolding a narrow passage in front of them. His wife was at the wheel, his newborn twin daughters sleeping in the back. This was their long-awaited honeymoon, delayed by Zoe's pregnancy. They had flown to Southern California from England to enjoy the sun and the warm, welcoming climate. Zoe was all smiles, telling him something, but he didn't hear her.

He sensed that something was about to happen, but he had no clue what—World War III, a massive earthquake, a tsunami...something. He was so scared that he turned deaf, watching helplessly as the car sped alongside a deep ravine and followed a narrow line at the razor's edge of steep hills.

Suddenly, he realized that in a moment, beyond the next bend of the road, they would crash into a huge boulder that had just rolled down the mountain. He tried to cry out to alert his wife, but no words came. He desperately tried to grab the steering wheel, knowing that in the next second, Zoe would see the boulder and make a sharp turn, sending them all into the ravine. He gathered all his strength but was unable to move. He was in a cold sweat as he saw Zoe panicking and spinning the wheel sharply to the right before letting it go altogether. The car broke a small acacia tree on the side of the road, paused for a split-second above the abyss...and rolled down.

Everything flashed in front of his eyes as he heard the twins' loud cries and Zoe's agonizing scream.

Dr. Crow opened his eyes to see his office at Nevada State Hospital in Bethlehem. A crimson sunset filled the window, casting shadows on his desk. He had apparently dozed off as he was totally exhausted. He removed his glasses and rubbed his eyes, trying to forget a painful vision. Although the incident took place forty years ago, its memories were still excruciating. Rescuers had found the wreckage and discovered him unscathed nearby. Because of his excessive height, he kept the car window open with his right shoulder sticking out and was thrown through the window into the bushes. Child seats saved the twins, but Zoe had no chance of survival in the heap of smoldering, twisted metal. He was a young biologist back then, a graduate of the University of Edinburgh. He had big plans, but Zoe's death ended them. He was crushed, contemplating suicide, and only the presence of his daughters saved him.

A brief knock on the door brought Dr. Crow back to reality.

"Come in."

His assistant Maharish entered the room.

"What is it?"

"It's the patient. We need to decide what to do with his body. Should we bury him with the others or separately? After all, he was almost a member of your family."

"My *dead* family," Dr. Crow corrected him. "Keep him in the basement for now."

"Yes, sir…" Maharish paused as he had something else to say.

"What is it?" Dr. Crow eyed his assistant. He remembered him as a foreign exchange student with shiny black hair and dark eyes. The assistant's actual name was Maharishi, after a famous Indian religious leader, the inventor of Transcendental Meditation, and they had to shorten it at the hospital to avoid confusion. What region of India was he from? Well, it hardly mattered now, for they had both grown old. Now his gray hair was pulled back in a ponytail, and his weather-bitten face was full of wrinkles.

"What happened?"

"Bad things, professor."

"What…things?"

"The Security Servants are closing in. They may be here by tomorrow."

"Well? These people propagate violence, and I certainly do not approve of it, but what does it have to do with us?"

"They fight science as the work of the devil, including all forms of medical research."

"You are exaggerating as usual, my friend. I am convinced that this is not so bad. You may go."

Left alone, Dr. Crow returned to his papers. After he buried Zoe, his world revolved around his daughters. He wasn't particularly religious, but Zoe was just the opposite. Coming from a Greek Orthodox family, she attended a church service every Sunday. After her death, he started bringing Kyra and Lara to church, hoping, perhaps naively, that Zoe saw them from above. He even tried to pray, asking God for help in protecting the well-being of the twins, who would no doubt grow up just as smart and pretty as their mother. To him, they were a "heavenly bridge" who connected him with Zoe.

All this came to a crashing end when both Kyra and Lara were diagnosed with bone cancer. He was told that any treatment was useless, and in the end he was left alone in a cold, indifferent world with two little corpses in his arms.What followed was now the memory of a long dark period when he behaved erratically, sliding into a bottomless black hole. He tried to kill himself, failed, tried again and ended up in a mental institution.

He spent two years there, heavily medicated, and turned into a vegetable. He would probably have ended his days traveling from one clinic to another if not for one thought that suddenly woke him like an electric jolt: *Where was God when all this happened—to him, to Zoe, to his daughters...especially to his daughters, those two innocent souls?* This manic thought had haunted him ever since, but he was clever enough to conceal his feelings from his tormentors. On the contrary, he used their tactics, making doctors believe that he had resigned himself to what happened to his family—that he had left the tragedy behind and was ready to return to normal life as a free, fully rehabilitated person. He finally succeeded, was discharged, and resumed his scientific career—for the sole purpose to prove that God, if He exists, is the greatest mass murderer ever!

But how would he achieve his impossible goal? Dr. Crow pondered this question through long sleepless nights in mental hospitals, and it dawned on him that he must do this by putting the Son of God on trial. By cloning Jesus and punishing him here on Earth, he would punish God, the source of all evils. The church teaches that people on earth, young and old, good, and bad, suffer for the sins of their fathers. Then why not make the Son of God suffer for God's sins?

CHAPTER 5

CASABLANCA

MEG STOOD ON A CLIFF, high above the waves of the Pacific. In the distance, seagulls fell one after another into its dark-blue waters, hunting for fish. Their screams, picked up by the wind, echoed through the salty air. A white sail on the horizon was getting smaller, dissolving into the morning haze. Gazing at endless rows of ever-changing waves, she reflected on her life. What happened? How did she, a popular student at her college who had already embarked on a successful modeling career, end up being alone, without friends or anyone else with whom she could share her thoughts and feelings?

Once on her nineteenth birthday, she had skipped classes and went to take a swim. The beach was bright and endless, like her life in front of her. Two middle-aged couples sat in the sand on a plaid blanket. The men appeared gloomy and the women were arguing whether it would be better to move farther away from the water, too cold for June, or to leave the beach altogether. All looked angry and bored, like those first-timers who come to Central California in the summer—only to encounter gusty winds, coming from the north, and unexpected rain. Locals knew it as June Gloom, an annual phenomenon. She felt sorry for these people who spent their lives doing tedious work until retirement and then tried to reverse the time in search of their youth—only to discover that "the ship has sailed."

She came closer and, ignoring their looks, pulled off her jeans and T-shirt. She now stood naked, enjoying the ocean breeze and sunshine. She felt that her body was absorbing energy, ready to travel into the future. Men eyed her in silent awe while women studied her features with envious contempt.

"I don't find her particularly attractive," said one of the women, who shrugged and turned away. "Don't you dare look at her!" the other woman whispered to her husband.

Meg ran to the ocean and dove into the reflection of the blue California sky. The current was strong and quickly took her away from the shore. Excited by the sense of freedom, she began riding the waves that carried her in their mighty hands away from the worries of everyday life and all prejudices, envy, and anger. She could continue this trip forever, stroke after stroke, feeling how the ocean gently caressed her body, cleansing her of all negative thoughts...

She didn't remember how much time had passed when she realized that she had swum too far away from the shore. It was time to turn back. The weather changed, the waves grew angry when she faced them. They attacked her, blinding her and pushing her underwater. She was a good swimmer and struggled against the current, at first not realizing the danger, but then it became clear to her that she might lose the battle. In short pauses between hard blows to her face from the waves, she saw the bubbling outline of the Santa Lucia Mountains. The shoreline was still far away—too far. All she could do was to keep diving under the furious waves, holding her breath and imagining she was a mermaid, her cherished character as a child. At one point, she missed the ocean's rhythm and came to the surface too early as she was struck by a heavy, concrete-like wave. The murky world embraced her and pulled her down into its silent depths. Blood started seeping out of her mouth as the ocean wiped it from her face, pulling her even deeper. It was so easy to stop fighting and give in. She was falling through the curtains of the dark world that opened in front of her, vaguely recording in her mind that she had begun to *inhale* water in sporadic shallow gasps. She no longer wanted to get back. Time had stopped...

What happened next? She barely remembered how some mighty force had shaken her like an electric discharge and prompted her to open her eyes—only to see muddy gloom around her, thick and cold. Another jolt brought her strength back, and with quick weaving moves, she returned to the surface.

When she came out of the stormy waters, the tourists were calling 911. All stopped and gaped at her. "I'll be damned, here she is!" said one of the men, aiming his iPhone at her. Others followed suit.

"The birth of Venus," local newspapers called the incident while displaying her photo. She had become famous overnight. X-ward, Peek-a-boo, and other social-media apps were filled with her images and fake posts, which promptly took on a virtual life of their own. She began receiving messages from fans and responded to them in the vast space of the internet. And, she had no control over it. This was painful, especially when Internet Reality users voted to change her name to Casablanca. Porn sites were chasing her and people out on the streets who recognized her asked for autographs. This was an endless and torturous experience. Meg considered moving to another state...and that's when an offer came from the tech giant, Eve's Fruit, an offshoot of the famous but somewhat aging Apple.

Meg became Eve's Fruit face. Company marketing executives felt that its traditional logo of a bitten apple hardly worked anymore as public tastes had changed. People wanted to see something more tangible—like the image of a young woman with all the attributes of a flawless body, particularly a peach-like bottom with nothing to cover it. These were the glorious years of technical innovations, artificial intelligence, and genetic engineering. A handful of internet companies controlled the market, and their capitalization exceeded those of many countries.

And then, the 2029 crisis broke out. Some say the source was the grid of big corporations, some blamed global overpopulation, and some looked for answers in conspiracy theories. One way or another, the internet all but ceased to exist, the world economy collapsed, and people were left to fend for themselves. Eve's Fruit closed its doors for good, soon forgotten, and so was she—the face, still beautiful, that no one cared to see anymore.

———

Meg stood on the cliff a bit longer. It was getting chilly; she put a jersey piece over her shoulders and went back to her log cabin under the pine trees. She walked along the ledge covered with pine needles, turned to the front yard, and saw a man by the front door.

"Hi," she addressed him.

He was silent for a moment.

"Hi," he said back.

Looking at her, Lucas remembered Hemingway's line: "She was built with curves like the hull of a racing yacht, and you missed none of it with that wool jersey."

She recognized this face…an Italian student, friend of her brother. Five years ago, he was already tall and handsome, but he was still a boy, somewhat awkward and shy. Now, she saw a young man.

"Lu…Lucas? Right?"

Their eyes met.

"Don't stare at me like that. I know I'm not getting younger," she said.

"No...not that...but, weren't you a blonde back then?"

"California style?" She managed a soft smile. "That's what people wanted. It's all gone—this is my natural color. I hope you don't mind."

"No... Actually, we call this color raven wing in my county. I'm...so happy to see you."

"Me, too," she said. She recalled that Lucas wrote her a letter once to express his feelings. It was a medieval sonnet, so old-fashioned and touching, she almost cried. But sadly, she forgot to answer it like many other love letters she used to receive. Soon after, he left the university.

"I guess I owe you one," she said after a pause, coming closer and planting a big kiss on his lips. "California style," she said. "This is for the Petrarch sonnet you wrote to me."

"You... you remember?" Lucas was astonished. "You know Petrarch?"

"I know many things, including classical literature," she said, almost apologizing. "Please don't tell anyone, they'll laugh at me."

"I know," said Lucas. Both smiled.

"How are you? You must be hungry."

They had a simple meal: a green salad, cheese, and white Napa Valley wine.

"Are you still alone?" he asked.

She looked around the room.

"Yes, apparently. Do you see anyone?"

Both laughed.

How could she explain what really happened? By all accounts, she had a happy life. She attended film sessions, opened tech conventions, and hosted parties at the Eve's Fruit headquarters, but her heart just wasn't there. She kept thinking about that incident when she nearly drowned. What was it, a dream or reality? Why was she still alive? These thoughts bugged her and affected her love life. Did she have affairs? Of course she did, but nothing serious, no relationships. She was more interested in listening to Lucas. After he told her what happened in Turin, she turned silent. It was obvious that something dangerous was being concocted. She picked up the L-shaped key on the napkin in front of her. Despite the demands of her modeling career, she continued her studies and was aware of what was going on in the tech world—at least what was happening before 2029.

"Silicon Valley is gone, as you know, but there is an ASIC company that still exists…." She looked at him. "It's an abbreviation for Application-Specific Integrated Circuit. They moved to Vega City. It's supposed to be a less dangerous place because of the agreement between the SS and the federal government to keep it free from violence. The truce is still holding from what I heard."

"Are you sure they are still there?" Lucas asked.

"Not really," she said. "The SS guards are destroying everything associated with technology."

"Yes, I know," he said, looking closely into her beautiful eyes, so dark under arched eyebrows.

As he moved closer, she noticed a small silver cross on his chest.

"Do you believe in God, Lucas?"

"Well, yes, I guess so."

"And I don't. How can *He* allow these things to happen?"

"What do you mean?"

"These cruel times we're living in: suffering, death, and destruction of our civilization…"

"Times have always been bad, Meg: the Black Death in Europe, mothers and babies dying on the streets…"

"Then, why—why is this all allowed to happen? Where is God?" She raised her eyes to Lucas. "It may sound naive, but no one has the answer—no church, no scholars. Why?"

"We may never know, Meg…" Lucas paused and put his

arms around her. Their lips met. But soon she gently pushed him away. Although her heart embraced the moment, her mind refused to accept it.

"Do you want to tell me something that you didn't say in your letter?" she asked.

He hesitated.

"I feel just as when I wrote it," he began. "Believe me, but now… I'm different."

Her face became cold.

"Just don't tell me you are on a mission from God." She attempted to smile.

"Why are you silent? You can't think of another excuse?"

"Meg, please…"

"No, forget Meg. I'm Casablanca, the same slutty chick from porn commercials."

"It's not true! Please stop!"

She took a deep breath and left the cabin. Outside, under the endless space of the universe, the Orion constellation stretched out its stars in a perfect straight line, and the black sky breathed on her with the gentle night wind. *Can this magical world be real and not an illusion? But what about the reality we face every day?* she thought. All her worries and petty grievances seemed to her insignificant in this vast space. She had to start a new life, not in the outskirts of her present world—a cozy, albeit lonely existence—but something totally new. But will she have the strength to do it? At this moment, it seemed to her that someone was looking at her through the stars—someone who could see her whole life.

CHAPTER 6
THE DEAD END

DR. CROW CHECKED HIS RECORDS, reviewing long years of research. Cloning was his key to success, and by the end of the millennium, he was ready to put his plan into action. An accomplished medical scientist by then, he had amassed an extensive collection of DNA samples from all the major religious relics of early Christianity: the True Cross on which Christ was allegedly crucified; Sudarium of Oviedo, the so-called "sweat cloth" wrapped around the head of Christ after he died; the Image of Edessa; the Veil of Veronica; parts of the Crown of Thorns allegedly placed on Christ's head before executions, and other so-called 'first-class' relics, which meant they were related directly to Christ. To his disappointment, none of these samples manifested any significant deviation from standard DNA replication. But one more and the most famous relic still awaited close examination: the Holy Shroud of Turin, which bore the imprint of the face and body of the Savior after his death.

In the year 2000, when many believers anticipated the end of the world and the appearance of the Savior, Dr. Crow had joined an international team, which received permission from the Vatican to analyze the Shroud. Although opinions of his colleagues were divided about the Shroud's origin, Dr. Crow was able to isolate a particular DNA sample from the ancient fabric. The new DNA did not belong to any human gene. Dr. Crow was aware of the challenge he faced following his discovery: human reproductive cloning was considered impossible because of spindle protein complications. But nothing would stop him now.

He selected a surrogate mother, who was a virgin at the time, and impregnated her with the new gene. At the end of the same year, she gave birth to a healthy boy. Inspired by his success, Dr. Crow adopted the newborn and christened him J. C. Observing the child, Dr. Crow sought to detect any manifestation of his true origin. All in vain, his foster son grew up an unremarkable boy with a somewhat below-average IQ. At school, his teachers called him Jim Quiet, not seeing anything special in this reserved, unsociable student.

Thirty-three years have passed, and the final evangelical milestone was approaching. Exactly two thousand years before, the Messiah revealed his divine nature to the world. He was born again to reveal the connection between God and man, between the creator and the human world. Dr. Crow was desperate, trying all the latest techniques, from genomic reprogramming to remodeling epigenetic marks, and yet none of these methods produced results. It was a final call, and Dr. Crow felt a great deal of disappointment. In the course of all these years, his mission gave him purpose in life; it gave him the strength to fight the meaninglessness of his existence. And now, when it was about to end in failure, where would he go? He felt he was losing his mind again and would soon return to the mental institution.

This prospect hung over him as Dr. Crow decided to take possession of the Shroud to study it in full detail. Perhaps then the Relic would give away its secret. He knew that the theft could lead to dire consequences, but it was a small price to pay if he wanted to achieve his goal of exposing and punishing the world's evil—and the One who created it. Justice will be served at last.

However, the planned operation went wrong from the very beginning. Instead of finding an empty temple, there was a caretaker who resisted and forced them to set fire to the building to cover their escape. The old man was apparently killed in the process by members of the international Mafia who were performing a supporting role. Dr. Crow saw the victim as another bloody sacrifice on the altar of justice. In a hurry, they placed the Shroud into a portable container, having no time to ensure the absence of their genetic prints on the cloth, and fled the country before they were caught.

Dr. Crow finally had an opportunity to examine the Shroud, inch by inch, and to take more DNA samples to compare them with his foster son's DNA. Despite marks left on the Shroud due to multiple fires during its existence, Dr. Crow managed to locate the spot where the Roman blade pierced the wrapped body. Contrary to modern crucifix images, the wound was on the left side of the victim's chest. Dr. Crow was bewildered by this fact initially but then attributed the discrepancy to the artistic renderings of medieval craftsmen. The wound was in the area where he identified what he called the *Divine Gene*, which came directly from the Messiah's blood. Inspired by his success, Dr. Crow chose the biblical way to deliver new DNA into his foster son by giving J. C. a gene-infused solution to drink, thus inserting into the recipient's DNA chain the Divine Gene.

And then, totally unexpected, disaster struck. As soon as J. C. took a sip of the drink, he fell dead, and despite all efforts to revive him, it was impossible to bring the young man back to life. Dr. Crowe was more than desperate, his whole life suddenly collapsed. Years and years of his work, countless attempts to accomplish the impossible, had ended in failure.

He was unable to recover from his final blow. In his arms now was another dead body, the life that he had sacrificed to science. Did he harbor any personal feelings for the victim at this moment? It was impossible, for all the emotions inside him had long since died along with his family.

Cold and unfeeling, Dr. Crow stared at his daughters' pictures on his desk. He was about to open the drawer where a 9mm Browning awaited him all these years, but then he remembered something and got up from the desk. He headed to the basement.

Fluorescent tubes lit a secret operating room. There, on a stainless-steel examination table, the body was covered with a hospital sheet. Dr. Crow came closer and lifted the cloth: J. C.'s eyes were closed, his hollow cheeks were pale, and his bloodless lips were pressed tightly together. The doctor pulled the sheet further down. The chest area was deathly pale, and a small vein on the upper part near the throat did not beat. His foster son, his patient, his last hope was dead.

"Can you hear me?" Dr. Crow whispered, looking closely into J. C.'s face. "Why did you do it to me?"

There was silence in the room, and the doctor knew that he was slowly losing his mind talking to the deceased.

Maharish ran into the room. "Professor, the SS are marching in!" His hands were shaking as he grabbed his papers, piled up on the metal table in the corner. "What are we going to do?"

"Are you certain about it? What's your source of information?" Dr. Crow asked, distracted from his thoughts.

"People saw them entering the city. Our ambulance brigade just got caught and has been slaughtered—to the last man!"

Dr. Crow paused for a long time then headed to the exit. "Follow me, I'll show you what to do…"

Ten minutes later, Maharish, wearing a pair of mechanic overalls, rushed back into the operating room. He heaved J. C. onto a service cart and rolled it into the hospital morgue. There, he covered it with a few dead bodies. Ten more minutes passed, and a service van loaded with cadavers pulled out of an idle railway tunnel several blocks from the hospital. The instruction given to Maharish was simple: *Commit J. C. to the ground and mark the grave.*

CHAPTER 7
MASSACRE OF THE INNOCENT

THE CENTURION of the First SS wing, Goliath, led his men through the streets of Bethlehem, Nevada. His uniform was coal-black, and the swords on his shoulder straps were like fiery arrows. His *century* was the leading edge of the assault force aimed at destroying the evil presence in Bethlehem, starting with the city hospital and its maternity ward. He had been informed that dangerous experiments were carried out there, aimed at destroying the world. Goliath hadn't been concerned about details—what exactly was taking place there, why, and who was responsible. The centurion only cared to know that all hospital staffers were to be destroyed, including women in labor. All science was evil, as far as he was concerned, and had brought the world to its present apocalyptic state. His men were determined to do whatever was needed to stop it. Their boots stamped the pavement, and torches in their hands cast red lights on the walls of the buildings.

His unit reached the central square and surrounded the hospital. They all stood still, watching as patients, doctors, and nurses rushed back and forth in panic behind the windows in despair. They knew what was coming to them.

A few unarmed hospital guards stepped outside with

raised hands. The waiting was ominous. In the silence, only the muffled screams of women in the hospital and the cracking of torches in the hands of the SS guards could be heard.

Goliath looked at the black night sky above, his soldiers, and the hospital, knowing that in a minute everything would change—and it depended only on him, no one else. He paused for a moment...and then gave a signal to his men. Torches flew into the windows, breaking the glass and setting the building on fire. Goliath glanced at the torch in his arm and hurled it high into the sky. Its trajectory left a fiery arc as the torch smashed the window on the top floor.

Dr. Crow sat still at his desk. He didn't move as the windowpane shattered and flames engulfed his office. He stared at the pictures of Kyra and Lara. Their faces came to life in the fire; the twins laughed, inviting him to join them.

"I'm coming, I am coming to you," he said, feeling for the grip of the pistol. His time had come. The shot was almost inaudible in the roar of the fire. The soldiers outside were busy massacring guards who had surrendered and women in labor who were fleeing from the burning building.

———

The service truck filled with the dead raced along the road, leaving the burning city behind. Maharish was checking in the rearview mirror if there was anyone in pursuit, but he failed to see the SS checkpoint ahead.

"Halt!" Emerging from the morning mist, a man with a 4-gauge shotgun blocked the road. "What's in your truck?"

"Cadavers—nothing important." Maharish forced a sour smile.

"What the hell is it?"

"Dead bodies. Corpses."

"Ah, stiffs. Where did you get them?"

"City morgue. It's crowded." Maharish kept smiling with wooden lips, feeling his heart pounding.

"There will be more stiffs soon, including your ass if you're lying." The officer walked around the truck and opened the back door. "Shit, it stinks here. Now, let's see…"

A deafening shot rang out in the truck. Another discharge of the officer's shotgun followed it.

"Nobody moves! Good. This thing can punch a 10-inch hole in an armored truck…or in your ass!" The officer waved Maharish off. "Get the hell out of here."

Sunrise lit up the horizon. Still not believing his luck, Maharish sped away and only dared to slow down miles later. He needed to check his cargo. Making sure no one saw him, he drove off the road onto a path barely discernible between the rocks and stopped the truck. With shaky hands, the lab assistant flung the back door open and sat on the ground. What he saw was worse than a bad dream. Pulverized by high-velocity shots and piled high in the cargo area, the deceased were beyond recognition. Blood, bone fragments, and pieces of dead flesh were everywhere.

The scene painfully reminded Maharish of his early childhood in a small town near Srinagar in the disputed state of Jammu and Kashmir on the border between India and Pakistan. Ethnic clashes between Hindus and Muslims there were more regular than the local train schedule; he had barely survived one such attack himself. Elderly people, women, and children were worshiping in the local temple when the explosion shook the temple's walls and the gunmen of Harakat-ul-Mujahideen started shooting and throwing hand grenades at the worshippers. Just one minute before, Maharish had stepped out of the temple to pee, unable to hold in three cups of green tea, his only breakfast that day. When the shooting began, he threw himself on the ground, right into the pool of his urine, and did not move. This saved his life. Then, after the security forces arrived and killed all of the insurgents, the gruesome ritual began. Together with the adults, he washed the blood from the walls and took out fragments of the bodies—friends, relatives, and classmates. The attack claimed dozens of lives that day.

It took Maharish some time to gather his strength. Wrapping his face in a kerchief, he set to work, pulling mutilated corpses out of the truck. Brushing off the flies, he reached J. C. lying underneath—and sighed with relief when he saw the body was intact. Now, he had to decide what to do next. It was out of the question to continue his trip. Maharish surveyed the area and noticed a small creek trickling between the rocks. Its soft whisper was clearly audible in the morning air. This was the right place to bury the would-be Son of God. He chose a narrow, grave-like pit on the bank of a stream and stood for a while, still not daring to put the body on the bare ground, and then remembered that he still had the Shroud with him. Maharish wrapped the body in it and carefully laid it in the grave. Then, just as carefully, as if avoiding to disturb the deceased, he covered J. C. with stones so that predators could not reach him. That's all he could do. Now, he just needed to leave and try to forget about everything: this incident and his own attempts to change himself by moving to this country. It was probably best to return to India, even though no one was waiting for him there. Then he remembered the last words that his master had said in parting: *Man cannot create the Son of God, because God creates BOTH—his son and man.*

CHAPTER 8
WALK THROUGH THE VALLEY OF LIFE AND DEATH

HE FOUND himself alone in a place He had never seen before. The sand under His bare feet creaked loudly like volcanic ash, and the valley in front of Him was strange and frightening. Where did He come from? And He…who was He?

To walk on the sand, hot rocks, and pebbles was torture, but this pain was nothing compared to what it was like before. But, *what happened to Him before*? The only answer He had was the silence around Him: no birds singing, cicadas chirping, or distant dogs barking. The fiery blind eye above His head burned his shoulders through a thin hospital gown, but this torture could not be compared with what it was before. But, *what exactly took place earlier? And where?* Silence… and questions, questions to which He had no answers. He tried to remember his past. There was a city… Yes, a city with white walls, towers, winged statues, and green laurel trees—many trees. But why did this picture bring sadness into His heart? What happened there?

Thinking about it, He walked along a path, which was a major road before, all but swallowed by the desert. Tired , He succumbed to weakness and sat on a boulder at the edge of the trail. It eased the pain in His legs, but when He attempted to get back to His feet, He had no strength left to do it. It seemed to Him that the volcanic rock absorbed all His energy. How long He sat there, He didn't know. Time stood still around Him like a silent killer. Waiting.

The sun was sinking behind the crimson hills on the horizon as He saw a figure in the distance. It was a man riding on something small, almost a toy. The man was approaching quickly. Then, the sound of a small engine reached Him, and the man on a motor scooter pulled over in front of Him. He looked at the rider with an old weather-bitten face and dusty overalls—and instantly, He knew every-thing about this person.

"Hey, who're you?" The man parked his scooter with a kickstand, took off his hat, and dried his balding head with a handkerchief. "Is this some kinda suicide attempt to get sunstroke, son?"

He attempted to answer this man, but no words came out.

"Are you deaf or something? Listen, we don't like strangers here, especially ones who ain't talkin'."

The old man stared right into His eyes for a second…and then the man's face changed, assuming an expression of confusion.

"I'll be damned…" The rider wiped his red, sweaty face. "I don't know who the hell you are, but I get every word you're sayin'. How's that possible?"

Dead silence.

Receiving no answer, the man started the engine, but then paused and shot a quick glance at him.

"No, I couldn't get more wine. Thanks for asking. There ain't any booze left for forty miles around."

The old man shook his head.

"Stay safe, kid." The scooter moved but then stopped abruptly. The man looked back at Him.

"I don't know who you are, but you're gonna die if I leave

you here. Sit behind me…" The man slapped his hand on the dusty cracked seat.

He didn't move, still chained to his stone.

"You're really suicidal, kid. What's the matter with you? Jump on before I change my mind. I mean it!"

The man took His hand and put Him on a scooter. The gray dust billowed behind them as they headed for the town of Nazareth, lost in the endless Nevada desert.

CHAPTER 9
HOPE OF NAZARETH, NEVADA

SINCE HER MOTHER'S DEATH, Hope had fallen into a deep, heart-wrenching depression. There was hardly a day when she wouldn't crave her mom's loving eyes, soft voice, and gentle hands that carried Hope when she was little and guarded her against the cruelties of the world later.

Her father was much older than her mom. A hard-working man, he was proud of what he had achieved in life and was keen not to show his emotions, let alone his affection, to his family. Did he love them? Probably, but in a special way, which was difficult to distinguish from indifference. Years later, he didn't show any sign of grief when his wife contracted pneumonia and passed away. For Hope, he became an inanimate object after that, and she ignored him. She knew that she wouldn't stay for long, and every day she planned her escape—and every day, she ran away from herself through alcohol, always available at her father's convenience store. "Wines of Nazareth," the sign said. There were hundreds of bottles on the shelves along with household items like mousetraps, paraffin candles, boxes of matches and even a portable blood transfusion kit. God knows how it got there. Nobody bought the mouse traps because, for some reason, there were no rodents left in the entire state of Nevada, as if they fled, sensing an impending disaster.

Today, she followed her daily routine. As soon as her father left in search of new supplies, she sneaked into the store using a spare key. *I hate this place,* Hope thought at the sight of dimly lit shelves and a stark room. It looked more like an atomic bomb shelter than a local store.

She took a large syringe as it was time for a "happy doze." The needle pierced the plastic seal and artificial cork, and wine filled the tin cup in her hand. She raised the mug to her lips and saw that something was wrong. The wine color was greenish, and its aroma was gone. Was it a bottle that she'd filled with her concocted at home solution after she had emptied it? How could that happen? Did she miscalculate the number of the bottles she used and those still intact? She checked the rest of the bottles, and realized they were all filled with fake wine.

Hope was scared and confused. Behind the thick walls and barred windows, she felt trapped, like she was in prison. How could it be? She was always careful, making lists of "compromised bottles" and those that could be sold to customers. She was so scared that for a second, she felt the floor under her feet begin to tremble. Then, after the walls around her shook violently and a rumble from deep underground filled the room, she realized *this was a nuclear test.* The jolts repeated over and over. Mouse traps, candles, and bottles fell from the shelves, and the antique cashier register shifted to the edge of the counter and dropped onto the concrete floor, its drawers bursting open and plastic e-coins falling out. A huge tremor threw her on the floor…

As they approached the outskirts of Nazareth, the road shook under them. The old man stopped his scooter and put both feet on the ground, trying to keep his balance.

"It's getting bad. These knuckleheads will kill us all with their nuke tests. Are you still there?" The driver checked on his passenger and didn't like what he saw.

"You really look weird, kid. Where did you get dressed like that?"

No answer.

"Ah, what's the point of asking? I feel like I'm going nuts talking to myself." They continued on their way and soon entered the town, a scattering of houses around a dusty town square. A few residents came out.

"Hey, Todd, who is this weirdo with you?"

"Ah, don't ask." Todd parked his scooter and waved to his passenger to follow him.

"By the way, I didn't get your name," Todd said when they came to the entrance of his store. The old man attempted to open the door, but it was jammed. "I'll be damned…the foundation shifted. These goddamn nukes."

The crowd gathered around them.

"Todd, who is this loony? Where did you find him? Did you get any wine?"

"Enough!" Todd barked and turned to the stranger. "They're right. What's your name, mister?"

Silence.

The townsfolk were getting impatient.

"This freak ain't talkin'."

"Get him outta here!"

"We must know who he is. He could be a serial killer."

"Shut up! All of you!" Todd was mad. He turned to the stranger.

"I'll ask for the last time: What's your name?"

Todd kept staring into the bottomless eyes of the tramp, and the old man's face changed as if he was listening to an inner voice.

"He says…he is…J. C. Yes, J.C."

Todd looked back at the crowd. "Happy? I told you he's got a name."

He tried to open the door again.

"Hope, are you there? Open up."

There was silence behind the door.

"Hope, are you okay?"

A half-dozen folks joined Todd, and together they forced the door open....

Bloodied Hope lay on the floor strewn with broken glass, an oil lamp on the ceiling dangled from side to side as another jolt shook the room. Pushing each other, the townsfolk rushed into the street in panic. Todd stayed with his daughter, gently wiping her face with a handkerchief. J. C. stood silently in the corner.

"How do you feel, Hope?" Todd said softly, peering into his daughter's face. Her eyelids trembled...and her lips moved.

"You...care?"

"Of course, I care...of course."

Hope smiled faintly. "You do?"

"Yes...you bet!"

Todd turned to his partner. "She's okay. Help me bring her upstairs, and then we'll take care of this mess."

CHAPTER 10
SAVING THE WEDDING SPIRIT

AS SOON AS his daughter felt better, Todd returned to his store, followed by J. C. They stood on the doorstep looking at the picture of destruction. The stocks of wine were lost, the shelves were broken, the walls were full of cracks, and the few goods that survived the blast floated in a huge pool of wine and kerosene on the floor among broken bottles.

"I'll be damned," Todd muttered. "I guess all I can do is clean this shit, but where will I get wine for the wedding? No wine, no wedding."

This event was extremely important for the entire town. Amid the gloom of their everyday life, the townsfolk had planned the wedding in an attempt to resurrect forgotten times. The town mayor and his longtime companion announced their desire to seal their relationship by marriage. Although both newlyweds were over sixty, their ages hardly mattered now as the ceremony itself was of paramount importance.

It took Todd two hours to finish cleaning. J. C. worked hard too, and each time he looked at Todd, the old man saw a silent question in his eyes. The stranger asked for a job. "Well, kid, I sure need some help in my store, but now look. Ain't nothin' left of it." Todd averted his eyes, trying not to look at his assistant. "I'm sorry, kid, I hope you understand," he added after a pause.

J. C. lowered his head, examining the palm of his hand, which he'd cut with a shard of broken glass. A few drops of blood fell on the counter, mixing with the water they poured on it.

"These damned glass bottles. I'll get you somethin' to wrap your hand," Todd said. "The state banned all plastic containers. How do you like it? Plastic pollutes the environment, they say…but which 'environment'? This shithole?"

"Here, take this." Todd gave J. C. a clean rag. "Anyway, there won't be any weddings this time… Maybe never."

The old man turned away but suddenly stopped and put down his broom. "Whatta you sayin'?"

J. C. eyed him in silence.

"Wha…what do you mean?" The frightened store owner couldn't help reading the stranger's stare. "Wedding? How did you…? Yeah, okay, if you want. Yeah, sure, I'll tell him."

"I'll be damned. Why do I listen to this man?" Todd asked himself, leaving the store and heading out to see the mayor. He was embarrassed and baffled that he had heard the words of the tramp even though the man did not say anything, as if they were playing some silly game for kids.

"What do you mean the wedding will be fine? Do you realize what you're saying, Todd? You just told me your stock is gone." The mayor got up from his chair, his face turning red as he banged his fist on the desk. "What's the town supposed to do? Smoke medical marijuana at the wedding?"

"We ain't got medical weed, chief," Todd observed.

"I know. It's a joke…sad joke, Todd. I see you don't get it…."

The mayor waved him off and fell back into his chair in desperation.

"He said…he would take care of everything," Todd said, knowing he didn't make any sense.

"And *you* believed him?"

Todd shrugged. "I had no choice."

"What's that supposed to mean?"

"I guess the town… We all need this wedding even though you and Barbara lived together for twenty years."

"Nineteen."

"Nineteen. The whole community needs somethin' to celebrate."

"Thank you for telling me this, but without wine, there won't be any celebration. Do you get it? No wine, no wedding. Period."

An underground jolt shook the office.

"Bastards," the mayor growled. "Listen, Todd, go back to your daughter, and forget about the wedding, okay?"

Upset, worried, and confused, Todd left the mayor's office. He trudged down the street and thought of the stranger he picked up in the desert and his ability to speak silently. He also thought about his daughter Hope and what would happen to all of them in this godforsaken place.

CHAPTER 11
BRIDE OF CHRIST

AS HE APPROACHED HIS HOUSE, he saw a bicycle leaning against the wall. It was an old European model with a worn-out name on the frame and flat tires, and it carried the local physician around town. Dr. Portnoy was waiting for him inside. He had already examined Hope and found her condition serious.

"How serious?" Todd asked.

"You see, there is something I need to tell you," the doctor dithered.

"Yeah, what?"

"I don't know how to put it."

"Then, put it anyway, goddamn it!" Todd had a short fuse.

"Well, I fear your daughter has a dependency issue, and—how can I say it—that problem underlines the seriousness of her condition."

"Meaning…? Hope is an addict? Is that what you sayin', doc?"

"Yes, alcohol, I am afraid. She needs close observation at a rehabilitation center."

Ah… Same old, same old. Todd immediately brushed off the doc's fantasies. He didn't believe him. Portnoy was a lost cause, living in a perfect world where his patients were expected to follow a healthy diet and exercise regularly. Thinking about it, the old man rejected the mention of his daughter's alcohol problem. He took the doctor outside and said goodbye.

"Rehab?" Todd told himself, stumbling down the stairs to his store. "I'll be damned. Rehab, my ass."

J. C. was finishing mopping the floor when Todd entered the store.

"You can stop now," the old man said. "No one's gonna come here no more. We gotta close." He looked around his store, which he put so much energy into maintaining. He saw bare shelves, crooked walls, and an old wine barrel sitting in a dusty corner as a reminder of his past success. "That's it, mister—we're finished. No wine, no store."

A soft smile lit up J. C.'s face. He pointed at the barrel.

"What do you mean, '*We got it*'? Where? That thing is empty. It's been empty for years."

J. C. took a tin cup and walked over to the barrel.

Todd followed him with his eyes, feeling fear take possession of him.

"Wha…what're you doin', mister?" Somehow, he knew what was about to happen.

J. C. opened the wooden plug and a red runlet filled the cup.

"What the…ho…holy mother?" It took Todd all his strength to overcome his terror and taste what was in the cup. He dipped his finger into it and smelled and licked the substance.

"I'll be damned." He licked it again. "It's wine. Very good one!"

He knocked out a bung stopper on the barrel's top and peeped inside. The barrel was full. Todd turned to J. C.

"Who are you, mister? Some kinda magician?" Todd continued to look into the eyes of the mysterious man, searching for an answer. The fear gradually left him, and the old man's lips spread into a wide grin.

"You just got a full-time job, mister. Get buzzy. Fill those buckets with your stuff."

Festive tables were set on the town square under a sycamore tree, the only tree in Nazareth. Todd and his new assistant carried buckets of wine to the guests, placing them at the end of each table. Happy guests scooped it with their cups. The wedding was under way, and no one paid attention to time.

"People of Nazareth, I have something to tell you." The mayor rose from his chair, which he brought from his office. His words were drowned out by the noise of drunken voices. "Hey, listen up!"

The guests became quiet and reluctantly put down their mugs.

"We have all gathered here not only for my wedding. You know it's been long overdue though, with God as my witness, I love my wife-to-be." The mayor nodded at the bride, Barbara, a local fixture who badly needed to shed pounds and years of her life to achieve a proper wedding look. "It's much more than that. We're out to make a point: We are not dead, and our town is not dead, although it may look like it sometimes in these difficult times. But should we surrender? People of Nazareth never give up!"

To the mayor's surprise, at this point of his speech, everyone turned away and stared at someone behind him in awe and astonishment. He followed their eyes and saw Hope in a white dress—thin, airy, and almost translucent. She walked to them with light steps as if floating above the ground. Her pale face glowed timidly like a candle.

"Bride of Christ," said a voice in the crowd.

"Are you sure this is she?"

"Who?"

"Our Hope."

"My God, she's so pretty…"

Hope bowed slightly to the gathering of townsfolk and sat alone at the end of a table.

"So, that's what I say." The mayor raised his glass. "Let us all enjoy this happy moment!"

The feast went on. Guests were singing, dancing, and drinking. Everyone was happy. The day quickly rolled to an end, and the evening darkness thickened in the desert surrounding Nazareth as someone noticed that Hope had dropped her shoulders, laid her head on the table, and was not moving.

"Doctor!"

"Where is he?"

"Doc!"

Dr. Portnoy was busy talking to the mayor at another table and did not immediately respond. He finally showed up and checked Hope's pulse. He frowned and checked it again.

The townsfolk looked at him impatiently, expecting what he would say.

"So doc, speak up. How is she?" Todd confronted him.

"She…has no pulse," Portnoy finally said. "I fear she's no longer with us."

"What do you mean? Make sense, doc."

"She has passed away, I'm afraid."

Todd stood still, then grabbed his head with both hands.

"No… No!!"

He rushed to his daughter and embraced her lifeless body in despair, trying to wake her. He peered into her face, hoping to see signs of life. He was no longer able to contain his grief, as he used to do – his love, his despair, and other feelings that all the men in their town were expected to hide to keep their machismo.

"Wake up, my love… wake up," he muttered through his tears.

"I think she has consumed too much alcohol—a lethal dose, no doubt," Portnoy said, taking off his glasses. "I am sorry, but there is nothing I can do."

"Who gave her wine?" the mayor asked, addressing the crowd.

"I saw her drinking," said someone. "She must've got it herself…or, it could be that weirdo who ain't talking."

"Yeah, he carried wine to the table," another celebrant said. "I saw it."

"How do you know this is wine? Could it be poison?"

"I don't feel well too," came a woman's voice in the crowd.

"Find him," the mayor commanded, "and take the girl back to her home." He turned to Todd. "Listen, Todd, whatever I say now won't ease your pain, but there's one thing I promise—the murderer will be caught and punished."

CHAPTER 12
RESURRECTED

NEWS about the teenager's death hit the town hard and turned the festive crowd into an angry mob. The folks needed a culprit, and their choice was obvious—the stranger who they figured had killed Hope with a potion. Everyone was horrified by the prospect that the wine they drank could also be poisoned. A few old women immediately felt sick, and the town of Nazareth revolted. People grabbed sticks and stakes, looking for the killer, but could not find him anywhere. The suspect had vanished just as suddenly as he had appeared before. The old women were convinced this was the devil himself.

Tired and heartbroken, Todd returned home to his dead daughter. He slowly climbed the creaky staircase leading to her bedroom on the second floor when suddenly he heard some noise behind the door. Someone was in the room, someone alive. What was this person doing in the dead girl's room? Todd grabbed a shovel and pushed the door open. Bending over his daughter, the fugitive held a blood transfusion kit attached to her corpse with the clear intention of drinking her blood.

Todd hit the criminal with the shovel, and the fugitive fell, drenched in his blood. Todd grabbed the tube, snatched the needle out of his daughter's arm, and threw the blood transfusion set out the window.

"Hey, Todd, what's goin' on?" someone on the street cried out. "Why're ya throwin' bloody rags at passersby?"

"Come up here!" Todd said, leaning out. "You'll see why. And bring more people, cause I caught the devil by my daughter's bed!"

"She was the only one I lived for after the death of my wife," Todd said as the mob broke into the room. "I knew she wanted to run away from here, but I was hoping everything would work out and she would be happy in the end…" He stopped, unable to continue.

J. C. came to his senses and slowly got up from the floor. He looked around; his blood was all over the room. "Grieve no more, father. Your child is not dead. She is asleep," he said. His voice was soft, and his lips barely moved, but the whole crowd heard these penetrating words.

The sunbeam coming in from the window fell on Todd, waking him.

"You…you know she is dead. You did it! And now, you're laughing at me, laughing at my grief? You are not a man, you are a devil!" cried the heartbroken father. Dr. Portnoy emerged from the crowd on the stairs with a death certificate. He checked the body and shook his head.

"There is no pulse, no reflexes. The body is completely cold, and the muscles have begun to ossify," he pronounced, putting the document on the blanket covering Hope. He turned to the crowd. "Take this man away!"

Mad with rage, people pulled the killer out of the house and, not letting him get to his feet, dragged him down the road to the sycamore tree. The people's patience was exhausted; the murder must be avenged! Two villagers with sweaty, angry faces threw a rope over a branch and slipped a noose around the criminal's neck. The crowd subsided: curses, wild frenzied cries were replaced by deathly silence, in which only the sights of women and hoarse, breaking breathing of men ready to execute the guilty could be heard. Minutes passed… everyone stared at the heartbroken father, waiting for his signal to pull the rope… as… Hope appeared from the house. Her eyes were closed as if she was sleepwalking, and in her lifeless hands, she clenched her death certificate.

CHAPTER 13
CATASTROPHE

A NEW DAY at the Area 6 Control Complex started as usual with a countdown to the next underground nuclear test. This particular blast was meant to commemorate the sixtieth anniversary of the thermonuclear explosion at Canniki, the biggest underground test of all time. Sixty years ago, the record blast showed the world that the US was a global super-power. Today, the new test was meant to demonstrate to the country's own population that the federal government was still in control.

The vast, 1,500-square-mile test site was sealed by base perimeter guards, and a chorus of sirens marked the final minutes before the blast. The Control Point technicians were ready. This time, the test was equal to fifty million tons of TNT, ten times more powerful than the original charge, and no one knew what the seismic reaction would be to such an explosion.

Sixty seconds before the countdown to zero, the guards left their positions and took refuge in bunkers deep underground. Everything and everyone froze in anticipation until the moment the earth moved, waking up desert creatures for hundreds of miles. A mile from the epicenter, a circle of steamy geysers burst out of the ground, and the earth took a deep breath. A small observation cabin in the middle of the test site fell into the opened chasm, dragging dozens of black cables with it. A huge boom filled the air, and the earth rose, shaking off antennas and control posts from its surface. The giant mushroom of an atomic explosion tore up the sky over the desert, blocking the sun. This was a nuclear disaster of gigantic proportions.

———

Meanwhile, dozens of miles away, the mayor of Nazareth, the townspeople, and the victim's father looked at resurrected Hope in shock.

"Y...you?" said Todd, catching air with his lips. His daughter opened her eyes and looked at him as if seeing his face for the first time. Todd shuddered. Instead of his daughter's blue eyes, two black holes stared at him.

"No..." the old man whispered helplessly. He grabbed his chest, feeling his heart stop, and slowly, as in a bad dream, sank to the ground.

Hope kept looking at her father.

"Cover her eyes—she's gonna kill him," someone cried out.

"She's not Hope anymore... Who is she?" said another frightened voice.

People were lost in confusion. None of them dared to confront the walking dead... as a huge orange cloud descended on the town. It came straight from the sun and scorched everything with fire. Everyone fell, pressed to the ground, escaping a massive explosion, which leveled many houses. In the mist of the dusty cloud that followed the blast, J. C. rose to his feet, took the noose from his neck, and walked away. Hope followed him.

Among the people lying on the town square no one had the courage to stop the "killer" or his victim, who looked like a frightening corpse on the move. Long shadows crawled behind them.

Vega City was asleep when they reached it. Once shining with thousands of lights, Vega Boulevard was plunged into darkness and its fountains went dry. The wind blew through the gouged hotel windows as branches of withered palms reached out to them like the hands of blind beggars. The Sphinx statue in front of the Pharaoh Casino stared into the universe in stone silence. The night was quiet, and their footsteps were the only living sounds in the city.

J. C. slowed his steps in front of a sinister building whose barred windows glowed dimly.

"Here." He turned to the girl. "You must stop here."

"Why did you do it to...me?" came the barely audible voice from deep inside her. "I...I was there with my mom. You brought me back."

"Forgive me, my child. I did it to make you happy,"He said sadly.

"You didn't," she said, disappearing into the streets. "You did not..."

"Forgive me," he repeated, reaching for a rusty door handle. He knew that grief and suffering awaited him here.

CHAPTER 14
FAREWELL TO CALIFORNIA

"HOW DO you survive here all alone, Meg?" Lucas said as they stood on a cliff, above the waters of the Pacific. Seagulls were diving from a height into the stormy waves, and their short disturbing cries, picked up by the wind, echoed through the air. "This view is mesmerizing in its beauty, but I would feel very lonely here."

"I am not alone. I have my books, my ocean…" Meg said.

"Yes, but…"

"And, I do some work at a nursing home for the blind. They are the only ones who appreciate my help and do not call me a slut for what I've done before."

"You did nothing wrong, Meg. Posing in TV commercials was absolutely legal."

"I'm not sure about that, especially now. After the Great Crash, everything changed. People got desperate. They are ashamed of their bodies now, and everything associated with the fine arts, nudity, sex, prostitution—they toss it all together without making any distinctions."

"It's so wrong. My country was built on works of art, ancient history… This all would be destroyed and lost forever if this madness continues."

"Maybe, but this is the new reality, like the destruction and killings of innocent people in the name of security."

"Come with me to Vega City," Lucas said, pulling Meg closer to him. "We'll find the Shroud together."

"No, Lucas," she said gently."You don't need me; your mission is more important to you than me with my problems."

"That's not true, Meg. How can you…"

She stopped him by putting her finger to his lips.

"I need to find myself too." She paused. "I didn't tell you about what happened to me years ago in these waters below." She pointed to the vast expanse of the ocean below the cliff.

"I feel that I was saved for some higher reason, something that would change my life forever." Her face became pensive. "Well, my life changed…but there is something more to it, much more. I need to find out what it is."

"We can do it later, after we get the Shroud," Lucas said, knowing that she wouldn't believe him. Maybe she was right that his mission was more important to him than his feelings.

"Lucas, you need to make a choice, a true choice."

"I know." He fell silent, feeling the pain gripping his heart.

His silence was a clear answer for Meg.

"Please don't continue. I understand." Meg brushed her fingers across Lucas's hair and kissed him. Her eyes were full of tears.

CHAPTER 15
HOUSE OF PAIN

PETE GRONOVSKI, a senior orderly at the Vega City Psychiatric Shelter, took over the graveyard shift. He hated his night duties because many things could go weird at night: escape attempts, brawls in the violent patient block, and suicides—lots of suicides. They were always taking place in the wee hours. The current shift was no exception. The trouble started with the bell ringing. Gronovski sat in a chair in the attendant's room, rolling up a home-grown marijuana cigarette as the metallic echo of the bell rang out in the front room.

"Who the hell is it?" Pete mumbled, he lit his cigarette and enjoyed it without moving from his place. There was always a chance that this was some junkie ringing all the doors in search of some shit to cloud his brain. Their neighborhood was notoriously bad, but it had become total hell lately.

The bell sounded again.

"Shit," Pete said, lifting his ass off the chair and putting out his joint.

"Who's there? What do you want?" he said, coming to the entrance.

There was silence outside the door.

"Hey, is anyone alive there?" He searched for the keys.

No response.

"I'll be damned." Pete unlocked the front door.

A strange man stood on the doorstep. He wore a hospital gown and no shoes.

"Jesus…" Gronovski examined the stranger from head to toe. "Did you run off from a morgue, pal?"

The man gazed at him in silence.

"Are you stoned? What the hell do you want?"

The man continued to stare at Pete, and the orderly began to hear the man's voice.

"Save? You want to save…*them?*" Pete raised his eyes to the ceiling. "All those bastards up there?" He grinned. "There are no saving jobs here, pal, unless you're mental. Got it?" He laughed at his joke and stopped. "Wait a sec, how do you talk with your mouth shut?" Pete examined the stranger. "You know what? You're weird, pal. Re-early weird! Hang on…"

He hurried to the attendant's room and pressed the button on his desk. An electric buzz echoed inside the building. Two orderlies ran into the front room, grabbed the stranger, and dragged him inside.

The Municipal Human Shelter fell back into its restless sleep, interrupted by the yells of distressed patients, the heavy steps of the security guards, and the clatter of metal doors.

In the morning, Albert Levinson, director of the mental shelter, came to meet the new patient. Well aware of the fact that he was too sensitive for his position, Levinson stayed in this gloomy establishment in an attempt to improve the conditions of its inmates—or so he thought. It disturbed him to see barred windows and bolted doors, but even worse was the anti-human treatment of patients by the staff: orderlies, guards, technicians, and nurses—especially nurses. Fearing every day that they might be raped or killed by violent maniacs, nurses fought back by slipping insulin needles into the patients' food, mismatching prescription drugs, and even poisoning those they considered particularly menacing. Levinson knew it, but there was little he could do. In the decaying city, the Human Shelter was not a medical facility but a prison and a dump for incompetent personnel and incurable psychopaths.

As soon as Gronovski brought the new patient into his office, Levinson saw instantly that this was not a case of mental illness. Despite his torn clothes, long hair, and bare feet, the patient's reflections were sharp, and his eyes were focused, although it was impossible to tell their color.

The doctor turned to Gronovski, expecting an explanation.

"Well, hello, sir." Gronovski took out a match that he was chewing in the corner of his mouth.

"He says his name is J. C. He's talkin' with his peepers— sorry, I mean, his eyes. It's weird, so I detained him. I have a keen eye for all sorts of freaks."

The orderly paused, expecting praise, but Levinson was silent. He could barely tolerate this man, a petty thief who was sent here for work rehabilitation. The doctor turned back to the newcomer and studied him more closely. Indeed, his most special features were his eyes, or rather their ability to speak. It was disturbing. Levinson took a questionnaire and handed it to the patient to fill out. Its purpose was to eliminate any personal bias in the determination of the patient's mental state. The score alone would determine his fate, not the personal feelings of those conducting the test. The doctor pulled out a vintage pack of Marlboros and lit a cigarette. The access to genuine, high-quality cigarettes, produced before the tobacco prohibition, was one of the perks of his position. He offered a cigarette to his *visa vie*, but the patient ignored it.

"Well, let us see what we have here." Levinson picked up the form after the man put it on his desk. He glanced over the page and, stunned, lifted his eyes at the detainee.

"What is it? You put 'J. C.' as your name, question mark as your age, and for the place of birth, another question mark. And, in the race section, you marked all the boxes: Caucasian, Hispanic, Black, Asian... Why?"

The doctor tried to find the answer in the stranger's eyes.

"Extraordinary." Levinson was lost, not knowing what to do.

Gronovski was losing patience watching the actions of the director, which he thought were completely unnecessary.

"Hey, doc, we gotta security quota to meet," Gronovski reminded him. "The town is full of lunatics. People ain't happy about it."

"Security has nothing to do with public lynching," Levinson said. "All citizens are equal in the eyes of the law."

"People demand justice, doc," Gronovski said. Their eyes met.

Gronovski clearly had his own agenda. The doctor suspected that Gronovski was sent here to spy on him and, who knows, maybe to replace him as head of the shelter.

Levinson went back to his questions.

"Are you aware of today's date? Put down the correct date, and I will approve your job application. Do I make myself clear? Answer me." Levinson was almost begging the newcomer to cooperate.

More staff came in, gathering in the room to watch as the strange applicant took the form, held it in his hand, and put it back on the director's desk. This was his answer.

"Is it your *final* decision?" the doctor said.. "Do you understand that this is a violation of the mandatory psychiatric test if you refuse to take it?"

No answer.

"Well, I did everything I could to help you." Levinson slumped wearily into his chair as Gronovski and his men dragged the new patient upstairs to the violent patient block.

———

MAXIMUM SECURITY MUNICIPAL PSYCHIATRIC SHELTER

Vega City, Nevada

Date of Exam: 05/20/2033

Time of Exam: 10:59:56 AM

Patient Name: J. C.

Age: Unknown (30-33)

Patient Number: 106786600

PRE-ADMISSION ASSESSMENT

Presenting Problem: Acute Psychosis

The following information was received from the Admission Office:

Psychotic symptoms are reported. J. C. manifests attempts to communicate through telepathy. J. C.'s behavior is described as bizarre. Inappropriate silence is reported. Ideas of delusional intensity have been expressed. Based on the severity of symptoms and interference with functioning, severity and complexity is considered high. Prior episodes of psychotic processes are possible and require more information.

Immediate Risk Factors:

Suicidality: J. C. appears to be minimizing the extent of suicidal ideas or impulses.

Self-Injurious Behavior: J. C. denies danger to self through suicidal, self-injurious, or dangerous behavior. Risk-taking behavior has occurred.

Family Psychiatric History: Unknown.

Infection or Disease: None. There are no indications of current infectious disease or recent exposure to an infectious disease.

Exam: Homicidal ideas or intentions are denied. Insight into problems appears to be poor. J. C. displayed oppositional behavior during the examination. J. C. was intrusive during the examination, exhibiting telepathic abilities.

Diagnoses: The following diagnoses are based on currently available information and may change as additional information becomes available: Bipolar 1 (current or most recent episode), Manic, Severe w/Psychotic Features (active).

Summary of Disposition: Admission to Inpatient is recommended.

Legal Status: Involuntary Level of Care Recommendation: Tier One Acute Inpatient hospitalization. J. C. exhibits severe cognitive and functioning deterioration.

Dr. Albert Levinson, MD, Director
  Date: 5/20/2033

CHAPTER 16

HEALING OF THE POSSESSED

THE FIRST TV Church of Vega City, or FTC as it was usually called, was going through a difficult period in its existence. Gone were the days of congregations in the True Believers Hall. No municipal dignitaries attended its masses, and even the core of the church's flock, its TV audience, dwindled due to the rising cost of electricity generated by old substations, untouched by progress. Fewer and fewer viewers turned their antiquated sets on, rescuing them from bankruptcy. As if this was not enough, the FTC spiritual leader, commonly known as Johnny the Baptist, had been committed for compulsory mental examination for especially dangerous religious maniacs. Respected before for his staunch defense of old TV church principles, Johnny had become so intolerant of competition that he ended up committing mass murder. In the heat of an argument with the pastor of the rival Temple of the Undocumented Prophets, too liberal for his tastes, Johnny broke into the temple, killing the entire board of directors. When the city police arrived, they found a grisly scene: the bodies were torn to pieces, mauled to death, and some were burned in a furnace. It took ten officers to subdue the insane man, and from then on he was kept in the most dangerous section of the asylum, where even the guards avoided entering.

Soon after the incident, J. C. was admitted to the same section. Pete and his people frisked the novice and dressed him in a yellow coat for high-risk patients. Then he was taken into his cell, just a few feet from Death Row. The cell was known to patients as the "Singing Room." Soon, he realized why. At night, as the dim light in the block bled out to near non-existence, the walls of the "Singing Room" trembled with the screams of tortured prisoners who were soon to be "exterminated." But worst of all was the hellish growls and satanic voices coming from Johnny's chamber, where hell seemed to have thrown its gates wide open.

"I can't, I...can't stand it," cried a small weary man in J. C.'s cell. "Let me out!" His arms were chained to the bed through the loops in his robe so he couldn't get up or even cover his ears with his hands. "Kill me!" he begged, beating his head against the bed. "Please. Kill me!!"

J. C. came to him and put his hand on the sufferer's head.

"Cry not...for soon your suffering will be answered."

The cellmate raised his red haggard eyes on him and then closed his eyelids.

"Nothing will help me..." he said. "Nothing!" He clenched his fists. "Please, please, kill me." He sighted, swallowing back tears, and fell silent.

"Lord, send help from heaven and strengthen this man," the words filled the chamber like calm waters, a quiet glow reflected in J. C.'s eyes as he spoke them.

Two guards in the hallway, who were checking the gate separating this block from the rest of the building, stopped.

"Who said that?" asked one, a hefty man with a military haircut, as an all-pervading voice reached them.

"Not me." His partner shrugged.

"I know…"

Both peered at the nearest door, a slab of scratched metal, behind the bars.

"Is it *Him*?" asked the first guard, lowering his voice.

His partner shook his head. "No way. I haven't seen him talking since his arrival."

"Me, neither. Finish the round, and I'll check on him." The big man came to the door, unlocked it—and came face to face with J. C.

"Take me to John," the prisoner said. His voice was soft but seemed to fill the entire floor.

"Who? That crazy churchman?" The warden smiled incredulously. "Hold your horses, mister. You aren't playing with a full deck. This beast will chew you up for lunch and spit you out as he did to the others."

"Take me to him."

"You're a crackpot, mister." The guard scratched his unshaven cheek, spat on the floor, and cracked a wide malicious grin.

"As you wish then. It's gonna be fun to see you dead." The man's eyes glowed with anticipation. "And I'll get you a thumb tag for stiffs after he's done with you."

They passed through the gate and entered the Death Row section. The barely lit passage between the cells was damp and musty; it smelled of blood. The guard and his prisoner went to the very end of the section and stopped in front of the "hell chamber," as the guards called it. It had no front wall; thick metal bars separated it from the hallway. The cell was dark, and no sounds were coming from it.

"I'll be damned. I hate this shit." The guard shivered and turned to J. C.

"Remove your robe. I want you to get in there naked." The man's eyes smoldered. "Go on, quick!" The guard unlocked the cell. He was thrilled to see how the body of this crazy inmate would be torn to pieces. J. C. paused and stepped into the cell without taking off his robe. The darkness swallowed his figure.

"Hey, what did I say?" the guard started, but then waved his hand. "To hell with you, we gonna' pick you up piece by piece tomorrow anyway." He paused, listening to what was happening in the cell.

Seconds, then minutes, passed, falling on the cement floor like drops of cold sweat. The warden still stood in his place and waited… Then, from the cell came an inhuman howl and gnashing of teeth. This was more than the brave man in the uniform could handle. Backing towards the exit gate, the guard switched on his flashlight by shaking hands—and saw the madman break the chain, grab the intruder by the throat, and sink his teeth into J.C.'s flesh…

"The crazed churchman broke free!" the guard shouted, fleeing down the stairs in panic, his screams echoed throughout the building.

Alarmed by the noise, Pete collected his team and headed upstairs, meeting on the way the guard, who was shaking with fear and could not speak coherently. When they all reached the top floor, they were struck by the silence. Not a whisper or moan broke it. They walked with caution and snuck to Death Row. Everything was quiet there. A few more steps towards the last cell…a few more…

"What the hell… Did you leave the cell open?" Pete whispered to the guard who trudged behind them. The man just nodded in response.

"Freaking idiot. I'll deal with you tomorrow."

"Y...you won't be seeing me here tomorrow... no way," said the warden under his breath.

A yellowish glow illuminated the madman in his confinement. Johnny the Baptist's face was strangely calm and blissful as he knelt and prayed at the feet of the patient who called himself J. C.

CHAPTER 17

MEETING HER DESTINY

HER LEGS NUMB, Hope stumbled after them. Night turned to day, day to night, and she barely registered it. She wandered through the streets like a lost object in a dark space. Was she really alive or half-dead, she didn't know. And what was "knowing" in the world she was in? With motionless confusion, she looked at the passersby. Who are they? Alive or just like her? They may think they are alive, but who can tell what they really are?

People were frightened on seeing her eyes, two bottomless holes. Most of them shied away, trying to escape her gaze and forget about the strange encounter, while a few others dared to follow her at a distance. Some tried to alert the police.

"Little princess, you can't walk here like this. Cover yourself up." An elderly vendor waved to her; his hand was dry and wrinkled like a piece of old cloth. He offered her a pair of sunglasses and was gifted with her smile.

"You're a beautiful girl, I knew that." The old man chuckled while fitting the glasses to her face. "God bless you, child."

She continued on her way, passing through the gathering of onlookers on Vega Boulevard. The crowd parted before her, feeling an incomprehensible fear that emanated from this fragile girl in her once-white wedding dress and black glasses like those of a blind person.

"It's a bad sign to see death walking," muttered someone in the crowd.

Followed by a growing number of people, she crossed the boulevard and stopped in front of an abandoned fashion store, once the pride of the city. Although almost all of the glass was shattered, one window remained miraculously intact. She stared at the mannequins inside, trying to distinguish signs of life in them. One especially attracted her attention. It was a girl of about twelve in a bright swimsuit on a tanned body. Her features were so precise and lively that she seemed about to laugh. Hope did not know why she kept looking at the girl; maybe she wished to be like her—cheerful, carefree, with a beautiful face. A loving family surrounded the girl: her little sister, father, and mother. It seemed nothing could disturb their happiness.

It was getting dark, rare lights reflected in the store window. Continuing to gaze into her own reflection, Hope made out two shadows approaching her from behind. She turned to them. The two police officers confronted her, flashing their badges.

"What's your name? Show me your ID," said one.

At this moment, Hope was too far away from reality and didn't hear his question.

"Are you deaf?"

Silence. Listening in, the officer suddenly realized that the suspect was not breathing. "Take off your shades!" he ordered, grabbing his weapon, a decommissioned Beretta 44.

When she raised her hands, he noticed a piece of paper between her fingers.

"Give it to me," the officer commanded, and his eyes widened in disbelief as he saw a death certificate.

The following silence was tense and overwhelming.

"All we need is a walking dead on our streets," the officer

managed finally, pulling out handcuffs. "You go with us, zombie lady."

They brought her to the city detention center, a stark, dimly lit room where hundreds of suspects, men and women, were kept for identification. Some were sitting on the floor, some stood still, some walked back and forth in anxiety. Hope headed to the far corner and sat on the cold cement. A ragged figure of a man next to her moved, waking up. "Ah, what the…" He yawned, spreading the smell of alcohol. His red swollen eyes circled the room and stopped on her. "Who're you?"

The man stared at her as if trying to read small text on her face. Then, his mouth dropped, revealing a few broken teeth.

"I'll be damned. You're that girl from Nazareth who Scripture says will walk the earth before the end of the world!"

He cautiously glanced around and switched to a hoarse, alcohol-saturated whisper. "Where is your master?"

She moved away.

"You can talk to me. Look, I'm on your side. Trust me, I'm your friend, and I need to see *Him*." The man's eyes narrowed and focused. "I am one of those who brought Him into this world. My name is Maharish."

CHAPTER 18
BORN-AGAIN MANIAC

CROWDS OF ONLOOKERS besieged the Human Shelter as rumors of the miracle that took place there spread throughout the city. Everyone wanted to see the fanatical killer who had turned into a quiet, God-fearing person as well as the mysterious patient who cured him. Dr. Levinson ordered all doors locked, not knowing what to do. Bewildered, he desperately tried to make a plan for a situation that defied any rational explanation.

"Do you know who I am?" he asked cautiously when the church leader was taken to his office. Two strong guards with sticks stood behind the patient for protection.

"Morning, doctor. I know perfectly well who you are, and I must apologize for the adverse impression I made on you in the course of our first meeting."

Looking at this clean-shaven man in a white shirt, the director couldn't believe his eyes. In his memory, he still saw the face of a maniac with bloodshot eyes and saliva flowing from his mouth whose hands were stained with the blood of dozens of victims.

"I gather I even attempted to bite you, doctor, didn't I? Please accept my most sincere apologies." The church leader displayed clear regret concerning the unfortunate incident.

How should I react to this mockery? Levinson thought fever-ishly. *This person was a vicious killer. And who gave him clean clothes?*

Up until now, Levinson was only waiting for the results of the psychiatric expertise, which without a doubt would recognize him as sane, in order to send the murderer to euthanasia. The city had no resources to keep serial killers alive.

"I see your dilemma, dear doctor," the churchman sympa-thized with him. "All your records testify against me. And yet, here I am—a new person, miraculously reborn from the flames of madness! Are you ready to kill this new man, to punish him for sins he didn't commit and trample all the good things that you have been doing all your life, trying to help the suffering in this sad institution?"

He seems to be laughing at me, Levinson thought. *What if he only pretended to be a maniac, playing his dangerous game and knowing exactly how he was going to win?*

"You committed multiple murders. Do you really expect the people of Vega City to exonerate you of all crimes?" the director asked. *What should I do? What should I do?* Levinson kept thinking, feeling that he was losing control over the situation.

"You don't need to do *anything*, professor," Johnny the Baptist read his mind. "Just leave it to the people to decide my fate. You hear their voices from the street? This is the common voice of the working masses."

This is a trap, and I'm about to fall into it. No, I won't let him, Levinson thought. He paused.

"The city council will render the verdict, not me and not the mob on the street," he said.

"But what crime are you accusing me of, may I ask?" The churchman pretended to be surprised.

"You don't know? You *really* don't know?" The director

was getting angry. "Has the murder of innocent people been erased from your memory?"

"They were *undocumented*, professor," the churchman reminded him. "No documents, no 'victims,' as you call them. Besides, as I said, the person who committed these 'crimes' is gone. Do you see him in front of you? No? The person in front of you has nothing to do with those occurrences, if they really happened. So, who are you *really* going to prosecute?"

"He has a point, doc," stated Pete, stepping into the room. "This is the position of our Council."

"Wh…what are you talking about?" Levinson asked.

"The Workers Council. We represent the blue-collar workers, the backbone of this institution, who create the values that you, doctors, exploit."

"What is this monstrous nonsense?"

"It's our new organization, and we are fighting against all forms of discrimination and oppression that we're facing," Pete said. "Soon, we will take over, and you will listen to what we, the working people, say."

A mixed crowd of disgruntled junior employees entered the room. Their faces were distorted by indignation over years of hopeless life and the most shameless exploitation. The labor masses were about to dictate their terms.

CHAPTER 19

JESUS 2000

AN OLD SCHOOL bus filled with tired passengers arrived in the city early in the morning. "Welcome to Vega City" greeted them. The sign was old, faded, and contrary to what it stated because the city was not welcoming. It seemed to be addressing entirely different travelers who visited the gambling capital of the world in much happier times. Getting off the bus, Lucas was stunned to see the state of this once vibrant city, and he marveled that any ordinary human could survive this destruction unharmed. Like most US cities, Vega City had its name changed from Las Vegas by the federal government's 2027 City Name Change Act, which sought to "rebrand"cities in a feeble attempt to improve their image. Of course, it did not in any way alter the trajectory of deterioration of American cities.

Following a lead that he received from Meg, Lucas located a large building in the outskirts of the city. The building was painted brown: its walls, doors, even its windows. This was supposed to be an application-specific integrated circuit or ASIC factory, though no sign would confirm it. Lucas waited at the entrance, pressing the doorbell until a man in a business suit showed up, unhappy that his work was interrupted. Meg's name changed his mood.

He smiled, and his eyes turned into thin lines on his round Asian face. He let Lucas in. Inside, everything was white: the air-lock doors, gloves, and the robes worn by employees.

Dr. Vu immediately recognized the key when Lucas showed it to him. It was a difficult task, he told Lucas, and it took them quite some time to develop the unique shape of the dual in-line package it came in. Instead of being through-hole mounted like most integrated circuits, this device could be inserted into an electronic lock and controlled it.

"Where did you get it, young man?" Dr. Vu asked.

"It's a long story, I'm afraid," said Lucas. "I brought it from Europe, and I need to find out who ordered it."

"Europe? That rings a bell. Let me check my records." Dr. Vu pulled out a small gadget the size of a business card. It lit up as he pressed the screen, scanning his files. He caught his visitor's surprised look.

"The technical progress is not completely dead, young man, at least not just yet. Oh, I found it. It was an import-export company, Holy Land. Never heard about this company before. But, our invoice—for quite a hefty sum, by the way—was paid by the Bethlehem Nevada State Hospital."

"Bethlehem? How far is it from here?"

"Not too far—about a hundred miles—but don't bother, young man. There is nothing left there."

"What do you mean?"

"Oh, you're not aware of the incident? The city hospital was destroyed along with its staff and patients."

"How did it happen?"

Dr. Vu's face fell as he told Lucas about the tragic events in Bethlehem.

"Well, these beasts will stop at nothing to destroy our civilization," said the scientist as he finished the sad story.

"Maybe someone still managed to escape," Lucas said.

"I don't think so. The SS thugs are thorough; they leave no

witnesses, at least not alive, and the fire they started obliterated the entire downtown area."

Lucas was crushed. His search began and ended with fire, and it seemed there was no longer any chance of finding the Holy Relic. He left the ASIC building in a despondent mood, trying to decide what to do next—go to Bethlehem anyway, or give up his search and return home? He remembered the faces of his friends who had put so much trust in him, who believed in his success. No, he could not betray them and surrender.

Looking for a place to stay as he drove, Lucas came across a billboard of sorts—a piece of cloth stretched over a splintered frame—that announced: "Jesus 2000 is in town! Come to see Him and make your wish!"

The poster looked like an invitation to a traveling circus performance, but apparently, this was all the city could still afford. Lucas shrugged, passing it by, but changed his mind when he saw crowds of people moving in one direction—to the black pyramid of the former Pharaoh Casino, where they were greeted with a huge, professionally printed sign: "JESUS 2000." He realized that this was much more than an entertainment for poor folks who were hungry for anything that might take their minds away from the existence in this miserable city. But what was it?

Searching for the answer, Lucas turned the corner and came across a squalid two-story structure with the neon letters "NONAME" on the roof. The letters "ON" in the middle were unlit, which gave the remaining "N—AME" a certain magnetic force. The building itself looked like it had recently survived a minor atomic blast, but something told him this was the right place. He was surprised to see a clean reception area inside. An old concierge behind the counter welcomed him with a friendly smile. His curly gray hair was neatly combed and he wore a jacket. This gave the concierge an almost professional look, but he still lacked something that would firmly put him in the ranks of hotel employees. Maybe it was the penetrating gaze behind his thick-rimmed glasses, maybe his independent posture, it was hard to tell.

Lucas asked the old man if he could get a ticket to the "Jesus 2000" show.

"You must be a California dreamer, sir, to ask for that," the concierge chuckled, referencing the shopping bag in Lucas's hand with "Napa Valley" printed on it. "All tickets were sold within minutes after the show was announced."

"Did you see it?"

"Me?" The concierge paused, straightening his tie. He glanced around. "Do you really want to know?" From under the counter, he rolled out a dusty Zenith TV set with a VHS tape player mounted on top.

"These things still work. I have a friend who was once my student. Those were the days…" The man's pleasant recollections caused his eyes to gleam.

"What about the show? Can I see it?" Lucas brought the man back to earth.

"Oh, pardon me…but of course, of course, please proceed."

The concierge flung open the door next to the counter and tossed a stack of yellowed magazines away, emptying a chair for Lucas.

"I am risking my job. It's against the rules to bring visitors into the office," the old man said.

"I understand," Lucas replied, placing a 20 e-coin chip in the concierge's palm. "And I appreciate your kindness."

"Thank you," said the concierge. "I'll accept it as a charity for the hotel's restoration." He turned on his antiquated TV set.

What he saw next on the TV screen confused him. A man in a dark monastic cassock appeared at the top of a dark tower at the back of the stage, walked down the steps, and approached a shallow pool in front. Then, he closed his eyes and walked slowly on the water, pausing in front of the audience. The man stood still; one could see the pool bottom under his bare feet. The water was glistening in the limelight, and the man was standing on the surface without his feet sinking into the pool.

"Well?" Lucas turned to the concierge. "Thomas Copperfield did the same. It also could be a holographic image…"

The old man stopped him. "Just watch, please."

An overweight balding man in a white cassock went up to the stage, bowed to the monk, and turned to the spectators.

"My name is John. Some of you may know me as Johnny the Baptist. I was the supreme leader of my church…until I lost my God, and darkness entered my heart. My mind was clouded. I became scarier than a wild beast by committing many crimes. I was caught and thrown into a dungeon where I gnawed my chains and spoke in devilish voices…until God sent me the Savior." John pointed at the monk. "Do you see him? Do you see the Messiah, whose face is shining at us like the sun? He is here with us, so do not doubt your faith. Don't be confused by those who hate our Lord for 'their name is a legion' and they have great power—but the power of God is greater than the forces of evil. God cleared my mind and saved my soul! *He shall save yours!*" John gestured to the congregation, and everyone joined him in singing "Hallelujah!"

A moment later, the show took a bizarre turn. The man in the dark robe *glided* over the water and paused at the top of the stairs leading onto the stage. The electrified crowd rushed to him, elbowing, cursing, and kicking each other. The stampede was endangering the life of the "Messiah" whom all of these people had come to see to ask for salvation. But people kept crawling and crawling, reaching the stage…

Lucas suddenly felt the urge to join the crowd in his mind

—to walk up to the "Messiah" and touch his clothes. It was dangerously hypnotic. He tried to fight the feeling, and his self-preservation instinct prompted him to turn off the video, but the concierge stopped his hand. "Just watch some more."

"Why? These people are obsessed," Lucas said…and then he saw something his mind refused to accept. The crowd pushed to the front a wheelchair with something that looked like human remains. The figure in the chair moved as the "Messiah" approached it. He looked at the sufferer with compassion. "I'm so sorry…" he said in a low voice.

"Heal him!" the crowd shouted.

The monk outstretched his arm, and then the parts of the body in the wheelchair began growing flesh, forming a naked figure. The disabled man opened his eyes. Other sufferers pushed themselves to the stage, and for these souls, a touch on a shoulder by the "Messiah" was sufficient, while others were healed just by putting their hands on those who were healed in front of them. Lucas was puzzled. Everything seemed real. More and more people had their wounds healed and praised the Lord.

"It seems quite interesting, doesn't it?" the concierge asked.

"I don't know what to think. Have you seen it with your own eyes?" Lucas wondered.

The old man nodded.

"How close were you to the stage?"

"Very close."

"And how many people were there in the hall?"

"Filled to capacity—about fifteen thousand."

"And, these people cured on stage…how many?"

"Thousands. And they were not paid actors—you could see how awfully sick and disabled they were before they were cured," the old man said.

"Are you sure?"

"Absolutely."

"What's the ticket cost?"

"Seventy e-coins."

Lucas made a quick calculation. "This so-called 'Messiah' is a millionaire then."

"His name is J. C. I don't know about him, but Johnny the Baptist, the one who arranged everything, is definitely not a poor person. His church was on the brink of bankruptcy, and now it's a prosperous corporation."

"It seems you're not their biggest fan." Lucas smiled.

"I have my reasons. I think that church and business should be opposites."

"Ideally, yes. And this magician—sorry, healer—where is he from?"

"No one knows for certain. He appeared as if from nowhere. Some say he came from Europe or something he brought from there gave him these powers."

"But what about this…show? Do you believe this is all for real and not some kind of hoax?"

"I only believe in facts, and we do not have them so far," the old man shrugged.

Lucas continued to study the monk's figure on the screen, trying to make out the man's face. Is this the thief who stole the Shroud and murdered his father? The one he was looking for? He turned to the concierge.

"Sorry, I'm asking too many questions." Lucas said. "Just one last one—are you a former lecturer?"

"Yes, I was," the old man said. "Let me introduce myself, Thomas Goldberg, professor of Applied Physics and Mathematics. My college closed its doors in 2029 like almost everything in this city."

"I recently arrived, or rather returned to the US, and I'm just amazed at the destruction," Lucas said.

"Why?" The old man gave Lucas a stern look as if he was back in class giving a lecture. "Is the situation in your country better?"

Lucas had no answer. It was clear to him that the professor was right in asking that question, but he wasn't just ready to admit that the whole world was in a terrible mess, including Turing and other Italian cities. He changed the subject by asking for a room.

CHAPTER 20

MESSENGER TO GOD

"CAN YOU TALK?" Maharish asked, eyeing her. She bowed her head in silence.

"Good, I'll take your word for it. I know you have some kind of inner connection with Him." He paused. "Do you understand what I just said?"

She nodded again.

"Say it. I need to hear it."

"Yes," she said, barely moving her lips.

"Good. I have something very important in my possession." Maharish looked around apprehensively. "This is His burial cloth. I can't explain how it works, but it's a *gate* of some kind, at least for Him."

Maharish once again peered into Hpe's terrifying eyes as if trying to see the afterworld behind them. "You are the only one who connects us with Him… You are the messenger…"

"Listen to what happened and why I know that." The former lab assistant shut his eyes, trying to remember everything that happened after he was ordered to leave Bethlehem and hide the body of the One they worked so hard to create.

"…three days passed after I buried His body in the desert. I already reached California, but still couldn't stop thinking about Him.

What happened to the grave? Was it intact or did vultures and coyotes dig the body up? Something happened, I knew it, but what? I could not sleep anymore, thinking and thinking about the grave. Finally I gave up and, cursing my sensitivity and ridiculous sense of duty, I set off on the return journey. Even a few miles before reaching the grave, I knew He was not there. It was an unfounded feeling that quickly grew into confidence. And so, it turned out, all the stones were scattered, and there was no one inside. The grave was empty, not counting the Shroud. At first, I thought they were animals that entered the grave, but then I saw that the Shroud remained wrapped up as if it still held the body. He had passed through the cloth. Fear and trepidation gripped me. I quickly took the Shroud and fled from there. I confess that the resurrected dead scared me a lot, but now nothing scares me anymore."

Maharish opened his eyes, awakening from the trance he was in.

"Nothing scares me, now!" he repeated and turned to Hope. "Not even you, girl." He shuddered, seeing Hope's eyes. "Jesus…" The former lab assistant shook his head, driving away the picture of hell that appeared before him, and continued: "I realized that I could not just leave. I couldn't disappear. I was appointed by some higher power to protect *Him*. But, I'm very sick, and I don't know how much more time I have left to live, but you have already passed the mark between life and death. So, from now on, *you* will be his guardian angel," he paused, catching his breath. "Put back your shades. You don't want to attract attention. Are you ready to do what *He* wants you to do?"

"Yes," she said without moving her lips, and her voice could be heard throughout the room.

After a new group of detainees arrived, police needed more space, so those detainees without a criminal record were released back to the streets.

"You can never be too careful in this city—never. Come here…" Maharish led his new friend to a remote part of the city destroyed by recent riots. They entered an alley populated by broken boxes, empty oil barrels, and strange characters who lived there. But even these people were frightened seeing Hope. Although glasses concealed her eyes, she emanated the terror that was felt by everyone who approached her. Maharish brought her to a basement, and they walked down a long, dimly lit passage to the staircase and descended into an abandoned boiler station. Rusty water tanks entangled in tubes and wires surrounded them. Maharish made his way through the scraps of metal and pulled a cast-iron hatch open.

"Here…" He stretched his arms above his head as if preparing to dive and looked back at her. "Follow me."

They crawled through a rusty pipe into an abandoned heating tank. Maharish lit up an oil lamp hanging on a metal huke near the entrance, he breathed heavily; Hope did not breathe at all.

Maharish glanced at her.

"You're weird, girl. Do you know it? I keep wondering how this could happen… No way any lab could create someone like you—no way." Maharish kept talking, mostly to himself, in an attempt to reassure himself that it was normal to be in such a place in the company of a living corpse. "SS guards destroy us and our work, but they can't destroy our spirit. Oh, they can't. *He* is here with us." Maharish choked and started coughing. The lab assistant wiped his mouth with a coat sleeve and examined the fabric. "Blood. Amazing—I still have something instead of alcohol in my veins." He laughed; the sound of his cracking voice was ominous. "What? You're asking… why have I become an alcoholic and drug addict all of a sudden? – Easy… it's the only way to blend into the street crowd of junkeys and homeless in this damned shithole. It's a dress code here, if you like." Continuing to talk, Maharish looked for something in all the hidden places of his home: in a pile of scrap metal on the floor, under a fallen piece of the inner lining of the tank where they were, and finally checked the old Holiday Inn mattress on which he usually slept. "Where did I put it? Ah… here it is!"

He pulled out a package wrapped in black plastic from under the mattress. "You keep it, and I will tell you what to do when the time comes."

CHAPTER 21

GUARDIAN ANGEL

UNABLE TO GET a ticket to the show, Lucas had no choice but to buy it from street vendors who resold them for ten times the price. This left him broke, but he had to get there at any cost. Lucas had no doubt that the star of the performance was the main culprit who committed the theft and badly injured his father, probably killing him. It was time for the false "Messiah" to answer for all he had done. Waiting in line, Lucas studied the faces around him. They looked frazzled and desperate, and none showed any hope for redemption. On the contrary, all these men and women were hostile to each other, pushing the weak, stepping on their feet, and cursing everyone and everything.

Getting closer and closer, the crowd moved to the huge pyramid and disappeared into its depths. The FTC used it as its new temple. The objective was clear: You must see the dark before you see the light. Would he see anything, though, after what he was about to attempt? In his pocket, Lucas squeezed the grip of a plastic pistol, which was invisible to metal detectors. Victor had made it on a 3D printer for him. Lucas's plan was more than risky. In the noise and confusion of the huge crowd, he would shoot the imposter to avenge his father, a gentle soul who might well be a saint. Everything his father did, no matter how small and unimportant, was part of the life of a simple man who had no doubts or contradictions. There were no good and bad sides in his character—only one good and honest man. It was too bad that Lucas didn't see it up until now.

The people in front of him walked faster and faster, rushing towards the passage between the giant paws of the Sphinx when somebody's hand touched Lucas's shoulder.

"I know what you're about to do…"

It was Meg.

"Hey, you, no cutting in!" The crowd forced them apart.

"This broad wasn't here. I've been standing in line since early morning."

"Yeah, them youngsters got no shame…"

"Meg!"

She fell behind as her eyes drowned in a sea of evil faces.

"I'm stuck here for the third time and still can't get close to *Him*…and my back really hurts. Lo and behold, I don't know how long I've got to live."

"He'd better do his job or, I swear, we may kill *Him!"*

"Yeah, enough. We will no longer suffer in silence. We must fight for our rights!"

Lucas stared in horror at the lost souls around him. These were the last survivors of the dying city, but where was Meg? And what was she doing here?

"Meg!"

The crowd pushed him into the entrance hall and carried him farther, through the ticket control to the statues of the Egyptian gods under what looked like a giant sarcophagus. The show was about to begin. The lights dimmed, and a soft blue glow lit the auditorium. It came from underneath a water container on the stage, no less than three feet deep. Everyone gasped when the figure of a man in a black robe descended the steps of the Mayan pyramid at the back of the stage, reached the container, and slowly, very slowly, took a first step inside. He stood still as if catching his balance, and then walked on the water to the congregation.

How is it possible? Lucas thought. On the TV screen, the picture was somewhat blurry, but now he saw it with his own eyes—the "Messiah" on stage was much more than an ordinary killer. Who was this person, and how could he get closer to him, within range of a shot? Lucas was making his way through the crowd, getting nearer and nearer, as Meg took his hand.

"Please stop."

"You? How did you find me?" Lucas was barely able to speak.

"*He* saved me years ago. I didn't realize this was *Him*, but now I know it...."

" You don't make any sense," Lucas said. "You're not becoming one of them, are you? Look, these people—they don't know any better, but you..."

"I am one of them."

"No, Meg, don't say that."

At this moment, the "Messiah" on the stage raised his hands, and the noise of the crowd subsided. He stood motionless, casting a sad look into the rows of heads below. The pause prolonged into eternity, it seemed. Johnny the Baptist rushed to the "Messiah" and leaned towards him, listening. The spiritual leader's face turned puzzled as he addressed the crowd.

"The Messiah wishes to know if there is...Magdalene in the congregation. Magdalene! He who came to save us wants to see you!"

Stone silence.

"Meg, what are you doing?" Lucas exclaimed as she took her hand away and headed towards the stage. The crowd parted, letting her through.

"Oh, I remember her... Long time no see."

"Me too."

The crowd grumbled.

"It's that slut from TV ads!"

"What is she doing among us decent people?"

Ashamed and confused, Meg went up on stage and stood in front of the man Johnny called the "Messiah."

A soft voice filled the entire auditorium:

"Your faith saved you, Magdalene. Now, find your life's true purpose...and go in peace."

The mixture of applause and angry shouts deafened them as the Messiah put his hand on Meg's head, blessing her.

"I don't understand. You told me you don't believe in God," Lucas said to Meg after she returned to him in tears.

"I thought I didn't."

"Oh my... your face has changed. It's glowing!"

Meg stood in front of him, exuding an inner light.

The "Jesus 2000" show went on as crowds of the sick and crippled besieged the stage, screaming and groaning to get His attention. Everyone tried to be healed first, pushing others away and not thinking about anyone else. Here and there, fights broke out in the crowd, and guards responded with kicks and blows, not paying attention to who was right and who was wrong.

When a particularly large mass brawl distracted the guards, a man in a green uniform got up from his seat, glanced around, and slowly, almost casually pulled out an Uzi submachine gun. The man took aim and squeezed the trigger. A series of shots rang out in the hall. Bullets sprayed the air above the Messiah's head. The shooter reloaded his weapon, aiming it lower this time as an inhuman howl drowned out the noise and panicked screams in the hall. Hope, with a white twisted face and black eye holes, pounced on the shooter, knocking him down. He kicked her in the face, trying to free himself, but Hope's dead fingers dug deep into his eyes, drawing blood. The now-blind assassin began screaming in agonizing pain as guards dragged him away. The show was over.

CHAPTER 22

PULLING THE PLUG

THE INCIDENT and the miracle of the Messiah walking on water under the bullets of the assassin gave the show a new boost. Even atheists and enemies of the Christian religion besieged the Pharaoh pyramid, trying to see the event. Inside, the huge atrium was unable to accommodate the growing crowds. Spectators were herded onto the main floor, and they stood in the aisles, by the walls, and jammed all of the open galleries up to the atrium's ceiling. But they represented only a drop in the sea among those who wanted to witness the miracle. And, in this desperate situation, the FTC leader found a way out by selling to the public bottles of "holy" water from the pool at 25 e-coins apiece. The cash registers at the First TV Church worked overtime. Johnny considered his plan a great success, and only the Messiah's growing reluctance to take part in the performance worried him.

The FTC staff were preparing for a routine healing session. Two men poured gallons of tap water into the stage pool, others checked the lights, and church technicians pulled on translucent strings under the water's surface, invisible to the naked eye. The "walk" on the water, after all, was the key part of the show.

"Listen, we need to talk." Johnny entered J. C.'s quarters in the pyramid basement. The church leader wore a business suit, and his sparse hair smelled of coconut mousse. His cheeks were freshly shaven. No one would recognize in this assertive businessman a recent maniac in a wire muzzle, feared by madmen and violent criminals alike.

J. C. lifted his eyes from the table where he ironed his robe.

"Your stage performance requires a massive investment, and my church takes this financial risk." Johnny checked the makeshift closet where J. C. kept his wardrobe. "Not much. I trust you are aware of *your* duties and great responsibilities in connection with this enterprise. All I need to know is if you are with me."

J. C. lowered his head in silence, listening.

"Good. I will take your silence as a 'yes.' So, you must not jeopardize the project by indulging in improvisations on your part." Johnny the Baptist paused as he often did on stage. "What was the idea behind calling up that young…nobody? You called her by a name she didn't recognize. Who needs this circus?"

The FTC leader took another theatrical pause. "Let me remind you: We have a list of prescreened sufferers, ready to be healed. They all had to wait while you were talking to…to this sinner, making no sense whatsoever. Where did you get the idea about calling her Magdalene? Is Magdalene on our list? Or, was she severely crippled so that her 'cure' would be photogenic? No. This person frivolously approached the stage ahead of the line and left the performance looking absolutely the same—no straightened limbs or healed wounds, nothing to be seen. What kind of show is that?"

"She is on her way to salvation," J. C. said.

"Ah, really? Only you can see it and no one else. Listen, you know what your problem is? You think you are in charge here, but you are not. You are a helpless vagabond that no one would look at without my participation. Let's take the last incident. Do you think this was easy to stage an assassination attempt involving a submachine gun and live ammunition? The former Green Beret practiced for days to shoot in the crowd without hitting anybody. It was a colorful performance, almost flawless. If only it wasn't for that wild beast that attacked him, ripping out his eyes... We're still searching for her."

"Who is she?" Johnny wiped the sweat from his forehead . "It's hot as hell here, but back to our business... I saw potential in you in the human shelter, and I chose you, not the other way around. I calculated everything. The punishment for attacking undocumented refugees would be mild if anything, but my redemption—or 'spiritual resurrection,' if you will— would have the greatest effect if the Messiah himself came down and brought me out of the darkness." Johnny smirked. "Do you follow me? You played your part, and you played it well."

"You are still in the dark, and your soul is possessed." J. C. said with sadness in his voice.

"It's your personal opinion," Johnny said. "I gave you the title of Messiah, so act like it. Do me a favor: Don't talk. I'll do the talking, you do the 'healing,' is that clear?"

"I will not... take any part in it."

"Simply walk on water and..." The FTC leader stopped. "What did you say?"

"I will not go there."

"Meaning?"

"I shall not take part in deceit."

"Wait a minute. Did you hear what I just said? The whole operation is a huge financial risk, and the very survival of our church depends on it. Running away, quitting, is not an option."

J. C. silently shook his head.

"Listen, you!" Johnny the Baptist paused and, seeing that his words were not having any effect, tried to change tactics.

"I see that this room has no windows and you don't have much to wear. We'll fix it. We'll provide nice accommodations, even a car if you'd like."

"I have everything."

"Don't say that. No one has everything." The FTC leader paced the room back and forth, panicking. "No one... I know you must be troubled by the deception we employ to make these people happy—to help them believe in miracles, in a higher power. By the way, not all of the crippled are fakers; many of them need spiritual medicine for their wounds. It is a white lie, if you will, to help all these people believe in your magical powers and be cured by their own conviction."

"And help you make money."

"Yes, we reap the financial rewards. Otherwise, how do you suppose this operation can be sustained? You have no idea... Look, let's take a traditional church. Why were billions spent to erect these magnificent cathedrals? Some of them took centuries to build and to decorate with icons and other images of God. So that clergy would live in opulence, you might think? No, these buildings had the same effect on those in need as what we are attempting to do here in far more difficult circumstances."

"Deception cannot heal; art heals."

"This is what you think. Many people think otherwise. In some religious denominations, it is forbidden to depict the image of God or the saints, even people. Why?"

The FTC leader eyed J. C.

"You see? You're silent—because the reason is exactly the same. Those denominations considered these images and prayers in front of them to be blasphemy, for no man shall imitate God, and no man shall worship idols created by other men. You may not know it, but even as recently as a few centuries ago, iconoclastic Puritans carried out massive mutilations of works of art in England and elsewhere."

"I will not commit fraud."

"Yes, I understand that, but can you walk on the water without my assistance? I don't think so. The church helped you do it for the sake of the poor. Besides, you've already done it quite a few times. What happened now all of a sudden?"

"I was…confused."

"You *are* confused now, Messiah, by creating a problem where it doesn't exist. Even as I faked my insanity, waiting for the right moment to manifest my 'miraculous' cure, you were the one sent to me by heaven. Isn't that a miracle in itself?"

The TV preacher laughed nervously.

"Do you seriously believe I was possessed and that you expelled demons out of me? You are a very naïve man, Messiah."

"Poor man, you are still possessed, and those demons talk now."

"You think you can get away with abandoning the church? *My* church?" Johnny frowned. "Then listen closely: I was protecting you, saving your life. Do you think you can survive without my protection? I gave it to you, and I can take it away—and send you back to the mental institution where you belong!"

"Poor man, your eyes are blind. He who has sent me is with me."

"John 8:29. Where did you get the Bible? I didn't give it to you."

"I know it, just as I know that you will be cured, but it will be too late. You won't see the light, poor man, and this saddens me deeply."

"Stop calling me a poor man. I will destroy you!"

The FTC leader kept pressing his star to continue the stage performance with threats and flattery, but J. C. remained firm. Gazing at the walls around him, he saw his future and the future of the man in front of him. The gates of knowledge were open.

CHAPTER 23
NEW ORDER

GRONOVSKI WAS FINALLY ready to fulfill his threats. The days when he had to obey the orders of every fool who called himself a doctor were over. It was time for the revolution—a revolution of justice and determination, where all shelter workers would be equal regardless of their education or rank. More than that, those who worked longer or harder no matter what they did—washed floors, took out the trash, or administered enemas all day—would call the shots. Pete's head was spinning as he imagined himself running the asylum and imagined Levinson's surprised face upon hearing about his resignation.

Gathering a crowd of his followers, Pete assigned them duties. The most important consideration was to isolate doctors and administrators. For that, his experience came in handy during a recent riot in the prison. With police batons in hand and stun guns at the ready, Pete and his revolutionary guards marched through the shelter, gathering doctors and head nurses, with none resisting or trying to escape. Then they tied them up, locked the arrested, and headed to the director.

"What does this mean? How dare you break into my office!" Levinson shouted as the attackers knocked the office door down. "It's unlocked," he added helplessly, falling into his chair. Pete stood triumphantly in front of his boss, enjoying the show.

"Now, listen up," he said, accenting each word. "I am the new director, and you will do as I say: Take your stuff, hand me the keys to the safe, and get the hell outta here!"

"I…I don't understand." Levinson pulled a cleaning cloth from his breast pocket and began to wipe his glasses, not believing what he saw.

"I said get out, or I'll give you a helping hand." Pete pulled out a stun gun and pressed it to the director's forehead. "Any questions? One…two…"

"Please, don't shoot!" Levinson begged, still not moving because his legs were not obeying. Pete grabbed him by the collar of his lab coat and threw the former director out into the hallway.

"Now it's time to put things in order here," Gronovski told himself, sinking into the large, soft chair. He opened a drawer and took out a fresh, unopened package of Marlboros. "Nice shit," he said, sniffing the cellophane. He ripped off the wrapper and was about to light a cigarette when a guard brought in his first visitor. It was the head of FTC, Johnny the Baptist.

"You?" Pete was taken aback. "What do you want?"

"I have an offer you can't refuse," the church leader said. He took the cigarette from Pete's hand and lit it. "Are you ready to hear it?"

CHAPTER 24
ARREST

"WHAT ARE we going to do, Magdalene? That's what He called you?" Lucas said, gently holding her hand as they sat by the window in his hotel room. The city outside the window was waking up in depressed silence. The ringing of monorail trains and the honking of cars were long gone. Only the shuffling of footsteps on ruined sidewalks could be heard as sleepy townspeople went about their business in the streets.

"He said I must find a true purpose in life, but I don't know why he gave me this name."

"I love you." Lucas put his arms around her. "And the last thing I want is to upset you, but…this could apply to anybody. Who won't need to find the purpose of his or her life? Besides, no one called you Magdalene before. How did you know He meant you, not someone else?"

"I knew it was me," she said.

"I see, but it's just that everything about this person, this show, is odd. I don't believe that He can walk on water. That is not right, as if He was playing a role in a bad play."

"You are asking things I cannot know." Meg sighed. "I just feel that I need to be there with Him…that's all."

"I was about to kill this man. You stopped me, remember?"

"You wouldn't do it, you know that." She looked at him.

"True, I wouldn't, but I still think He has something to do with the theft of the Shroud. Did you hear those rumors about the Bethlehem hospital medical experiments?"

"It may be the work of that sleazy man, Johnny, to promote his show."

"Possibly, but the company you gave me said the Bethlehem hospital ordered the key."

"Then we should go to the police," she said. "It's their responsibility to find those who did it."

"No." Lucas shook his head. "It won't help, but instead we…"

A knock on the door interrupted him.

"Who is it?" Lucas asked.

"Mr. Amato, I have important news."

The concierge stepped in.

"Oh, I'm sorry," the old man hesitated, seeing Meg. "I didn't know you weren't alone."

"It's…my close friend Meg," Lucas said. "You can talk freely. Is this about Him?"

"This is about the show."

"And?"

"Well, they closed it down."

"What? When?"

"Effective immediately, the announcement said."

"That's impossible." Lucas was stunned. "The show is sold out two months in advance. You told me this."

"I know. I don't comprehend it myself. Apparently, something happened to the star of the show—some call him the Messiah, some Jesus 2000. He is in custody now."

"In custody?" Lucas was stunned. "What can we do?"

"I don't think we can do much." The concierge shrugged.

"We need to get the facts first—what exactly happened and why."

"How?"

"I may know where we can get information," the concierge said. "It's called the *Vega Star*."

"What is it?"

"The local news source. My former students run it."

"This city has…its paper?" Lucas was surprised. "A free press is banned everywhere, and even official publications have gone bankrupt, but you're telling me that this city enjoys the luxury of having its own newspaper?"

"Well, it's not quite a newspaper, *per se*, but as close as you can get to it."

"Can we see it?" Meg asked. "We cannot sit here and do nothing."

The former professor eyed them, deciding whether his new friends could be fully trusted.

The Vega Star turned out to be a revived pager service. A group of unemployed journalists used it to distribute their reports. Anyone who still owned a pager could join the readership. The professor took Lucas and Meg to the *Vega Star* headquarters that was located in an abandoned city aquarium where they learned what happened:

WORKERS COUNCIL DEPOSES CITY ADMINIS-
TRATION
JESUS 2000 ARRESTED

BREAKING NEWS:
SS GUARDS ENTER VEGA CITY, TAKING
CONTROL

CITY POPULATION HAS 24 HOURS TO
SURRENDER PERSONAL WEAPONS

DOCTORS, ENGINEERS, SCIENTISTS, AND ALL
WITH HIGHER EDUCATION MUST PASS LOYALTY
TEST

DRESSES AND FIGURE-HUGGING WOMEN'S
CLOTHING PROHIBITED

From these reports, Lucas and Meg learned that the arrested Messiah was sent back to the Human Shelter. New authorities consider Him a security threat.

CHAPTER 25
BACK TO THE HOUSE
OF PAIN

BLOCK 27 of the Human Shelter had a sinister reputation. It housed sadistic killers; masochistic self-eaters with bitten-off fingers and severed ears; ferocious necrophiliacs and rapists; vicious human organ thieves, and many others whose lives were spared by the administration for observation purposes.

Gronovski had personally brought to that block the one who the city folks called the Messiah.

"I remember your face," Pete said, chaining J. C. by the arms and legs to the cement wall. "I saw who you are right away, faster than all these doctors. You are more dangerous than anyone in this cellblock. You think you're special? Take a look. All these creatures are your buddies now. Get used to them." Locking the cell and heading back to his office, Pete was proud of his new duties.

Chained to the wall so that He could hardly breathe, He looked around and saw a dozen pairs of eyes burning with hatred. They slowly approached.

"You took my spot," hissed a man with a severed nose. "You will pay for it." He rummaged through the rags on the floor and pulled out a knife made from the handle of a table-spoon. "You thought I got no knife?"

The madman brought the knife to the newcomer's face. "I like your nose. Should I taste it? Or will it be your ears; they look so delicious, like a human Christmas cake. Oh, I like human cake…" He paused, unable to decide where to start first, and after a hesitant moment began cutting off his own lips, blood gushed onto his chest. Someone in the corner roared in amusement. Wild, deafening laughter swept through the cell. A second inmate beat his neighbor on the head in total delight, a third rolled on the floor in a fit of fun, and a fourth tried to gouge out a cellmate's eyes, making him laugh even louder. It was a carnival of blood and dangerous, uncontrollable joy.

Witnessing this, He bowed his head. *Poor souls lost in the dark, they are trapped,* He thought. *No force can bring them to light. Demons cannot be driven out of them, for they **are** demons themselves, and they torture themselves.*

BREAKING NEWS:

SS GUARDS TAKE OVER CUSTODY OF J. C. SUSPECTED OF PROMULGATING RELIGIOUS OBSCURANTISM, DESTRUCTION OF SOCIAL ORDER

HIGH PREFECT OF CALIFORNIA AND NEVADA MARCUS ORDERS TRIAL OF SUSPECT

HIGH PREFECT TO CHAIR TRIBUNAL

F.T.C. LEADER JOHN AND HUMAN SHELTER DIRECTOR GRONOVSKI APPOINTED ASSISTANT JUDGES

TRIAL TO TAKE PLACE IN CAESAR COLOSSEUM:
ADMISSION 100 E-COINS

CHAPTER 26
LAST JUDGMENT

LOCATED on the once-thriving Vega Strip, the Caesar Colosseum casino had a murky and turbulent past. Built seventy years earlier, it was an attempt to replicate the greatness of the original Colosseum amphitheater in Rome with its huge arena and statues of gods, goddesses, and Roman symbols. And just as the arena in Ancient Rome, stained with the blood of gladiators, the walls of the casino have seen many deaths, including its shady owner, who died at the gambling table on its floor. Some say of heart attack, some – of poison like it often happened with warring rivals in the ancient Roman times. Now in this building, darkened and dilapidated after the crisis, residents of Vega City were to witness another large-scale event - the trial of the so-called "False Messiah," whose fate, like the fate of the first Christians in Ancient Rome, was to be decided in the Colosseum.

The bronze statue of Julius Caesar stared at Lucas and Meg with empty eye sockets as they moved with the crowd inside the main building. SS guards in brown uniforms met them there; soldiers were stationed everywhere—in the front hall and passages and on the marble stairs and balconies. Above them, SS flags tumbled down between the columns in long crimson swaths. The entrance to the indoor arena was out of bounds to the general public. That was where the trial was to take place, and only the court personnel, the prosecution witnesses, and city dignitaries occupied it. Average folks were directed instead into the vast adjacent open area, a former sports pavilion. It was filled to capacity with fifty thousand spectators. In anticipation of the show, people sat on the yellowing grass, eating snacks and yawning. Most of the folks seemed indifferent to who the accused was and what the charge was. All they wanted was some sort of entertainment in the godforsaken city.

Lucas and Meg found a spot on the grass in the inhospitable crowd. Time slowly passed by. A fat woman on the left opened her sleepy eyes on her red cheeky face. Eyeing the intruders, she reached for a soiled bag and fished out a chicken drumstick. Chewing her snack, the woman kept glaring at Meg, obviously angry that she dared to possess such a slender figure. Feeling uncomfortable, Meg turned away, only to be met by the dirty stare of an old man next to her. He had a long hanging nose and watery eyes that gleamed with lust. He could barely resist the urge to fondle his young neighbor's "fruits."

"Hey, get a grip on yourself," Lucas said, positioning himself between them.

It was getting dark. A giant screen above them came to life. It showed the insides of the Colosseum: crimson flags, tiers of seats filled with city dignitaries, and the empty arena in the middle. Long minutes passed, no one showed up, and the crowds began to grumble, and then slowly the mumbling became louder with cries demanding the show.

"Enough waiting! I wasted all my money on this crap!"

"Hey, wake up over there, we want Meal'n'Real!"

"Anybody home? Wake up!"

"Just what the hell are they doing there?"

The arena on the screen remained blank. Meg's neighbor on the right gave her a quick sideways glance and began to fumble in his pants.

"Let's go, I can't stay here…" Meg said.

They were about to leave as guards on the screen rolled out a massive metal cage with someone wrapped in a gray canvas inside. Three men appeared on the podium at the center of the main tier: Prefect Marcus, a tall pale-faced officer in an SS uniform with a Roman cloak draped over his shoulders, Johnny the Baptist in a black hooded robe, and Pete Gronovski in a silly checkered jacket who felt visibly insecure in front of the crowd. The judges took their seats.

The old man next to Meg and Lucas meanwhile kept exploring his pants, breathing heavily.

"Cut it out, or I'll knock your head off," Lucas snapped, turning to the pervert.

Back in the arena, Prefect Marcus raised his arm. "Reveal the face of the accused!" he said in a loud, commanding voice.

Two guards stepped into the cage and yanked the cover off. Meg and Lucas gasped. Instead of the Messiah's luminous face in a halo of falling waves of light-brown hair, they saw a thin, bold-cut man in a prison jacket. His eyes were dim and his shoulders sagged. The defendant clearly didn't understand what was going on and smiled helplessly, gazing up beyond his cage and the walls of the Colosseum.

"What did they do to Him? He looks like a death-camp inmate," Meg whispered in terror.

The Prefect turned his long cold face to the defendant. "What is your name?"

The man in the cage kept smiling, circling the stage with his eyes.

"I know you can talk," said the chairman. "Don't try to get away from the answer. Tell me your name."

"People call me J. C. That's all I know." His voice was deep yet distant as if He was far away.

The pager in Lucas's pocket came to life. "LAST JUDG-MENT IN SESSION" read the screen.

"Do you understand the charges against you?" the Prefect continued.

"No."

"You must address the Chief Justice as 'Hegemon' or 'your Clemency,'" said the Prefect. "Do you understand the accusations that brought you here?"

"No."

Marcus turned to the secretary seated behind the judges.

"Read his charges."

The secretary, a stocky man in metal-rimmed glasses, stepped forward and opened a thick ledger.

"The suspect known to the court under the alias J. C. of undetermined age, race, and residence is brought to court to stand trial on multiple charges. The defendant is indicted for planning and executing a series of performances in Vega City in the course of which he created an illusion of walking on water in a fraudulent manner, attempting to convince the spectators that he is the Messiah sent by God. These criminal acts allowed the suspect to misappropriate large sums of money and to spread his influence among the city's population, as well as in its administrative structures and religious organizations. Based on this information, the suspect known as J. C. is charged with aggravated misrepresentation, racketeering, and money laundering."

"What crap!" Lucas said.

"And I don't understand how that cleric, Johnny or whatever his name is…how he could be a judge if he set up these sessions himself and enriched himself from them." Meg shook her head in disbelief.

"Charging spectators 100 e-coins each fifty thousand, he's making more money than ever before," said Lucas. "This is his new scheme. The trial and admission fees bring in more money than any healing."

The secretary on the screen continued to read the protocol, page after page, and the viewers outside became bored. They had expected entertainment, action, violence— anything but this tedious account of charges that no one clearly understood or cared about. The angry folks returned to eating, drinking, and arguing among themselves. The old man next to Lucas snuck his hand behind his back towards Meg and grabbed her bosom. Meg twitched in shock and slapped the offender with such force that he fell flat on the ground.

"Look, this broad's beating up an old man!" someone screamed.

"Where, who?"

"That bitch dressed like a prostitute!"

The fat neighbor on their left tossed away a chicken breast she was devouring and pushed herself towards Meg. "I remember you now—you are that whore from TV!" the woman yelled. "You came here to rough up decent people, eh, bitch?"

"Whatta you waiting for? Beat the shit out of her so she'll remember!" someone shouted.

The crowd of spectators turned into a hostile mob as faces, distorted with hate, surrounded them.

Lucas jumped to his feet, reaching for his pocket.

"Don't move or I'll shoot!" he yelled. His eyes met the angry faces point-blank. "I mean it. Who's first?"

The mob backed off, grumbling and cursing. Lucas grabbed Meg's hand, and they ran to the exit.

"I thought they would tear us apart." Meg sighed with relief as they left the pavilion. "You are a real hero."

"I wish," Lucas chuckled, pulling out his pager. "It's not a gun, but it worked."

"You are very sweet." Meg's eyes twinkled.

"Here you are! I am looking for you," the concierge interrupted the tender moment. "What's the matter? You both look…odd."

"Nothing, just a little incident," Lucas said, slipping the pager back into his pocket.

"Splendid. I happened to obtain three passes for us to observe the court proceedings from a top gallery."

"You still speak as a professor sometimes." Lucas chuckled. "Did you notice?"

"I don't deny this." The former professor smiled.

"I don't believe you were properly introduced," Lucas added. "It seems that not only does your hotel have no name, but its employees are wearing no nametags."

"Unnecessary formalities," Goldberg said and turned to Meg. "Thomas."

"It's a pleasure to meet you, Mr. Thomas," she said.

"Please, no mister or professor, just Thomas."

"It's a pleasure to meet you, Thomas." Meg smiled.

"Likewise." Thomas bowed deeply.

They ascended the stairs to the gallery and took their seats in the uppermost section of the enormous Colosseum. By that time, the secretary had finished reading the charges, and the court proceeded to question witnesses for the prosecution. Johnny the Baptist was the first to be called. The church leader rose from the judge's chair and declared that he had personally hired the defendant as a motivational speaker to show the audience the breadth of human mental and physical capabilities. The "Jesus 2000" show was staged purely as entertainment and under no circumstances performed any medical or educational purposes, he said. He added that the defendant, however, using various tricks, perverted the purpose of the performance, turning it into a religious cult gathering with the aim of extorting money from the public.

"To my utmost regret, I had not discovered this immediately and had not closed the show before sending the defendant back to the confinement of the mental institution, where he belongs." Johnny the Baptist ended his speech with a sigh of contrition and tears in his eyes. "I am guilty of negligence, and I shall ask the Lord and all of you for forgiveness."

"I've sinned, my Lord!" The church businessman suddenly cried out, raising his hands to the sky and choking on his tears.

The audience burst into applause.

"What are they happy about?" Lucas asked. "That the main crook covered his tracks? Professor—sorry, Thomas… How do they allow a witness and a judge to be the same person? How is this possible?"

Thomas gave him a sad look. "Oh, anything is possible in this city, you will see."

"I think Johnny is the first who should be investigated," Lucas said.

"Perpetrators often become prosecutors to place blame on others. But, this is only the beginning. It will get much worse, I promise you." The old professor glanced at the arena below. "Much worse."

"It's horrible," Meg said.

Gronovski, who was introduced as the Healthcare Workers Council leader, was the second witness for the prosecution.

"Yeah, well…" he began, wiping his sweaty face with the sleeve of his jacket, "it was me who first met him that night. I mean, when he just came to town. He spoke in voices or he wasn't speaking at all. He's mental, I saw it. I says, 'Gimme your ID.' He says, 'Neh-ha, nothing'. Then, the doc came. Same sh…stuff. He didn't even dig what year it was. It was weird. We oughta keep him off the streets, that's my take—or what you people call it, diagnosis."

"What a pathetic creature!" Lucas whispered to Thomas. "Is he really a healthcare worker?"

"This man is much more than that. He is an illegitimate son of the former head of the City Council." Thomas closed his eyes. "I am so tired of seeing this... *O tempora, o mores!*"

Lucas turned to Meg. "It's Latin, it means..."

"*Oh, what times!*" she said. "I know."

Meanwhile, silence fell on the arena below. One could hear the crackling of torches in the hands of the guards and the creak of their leather boots. The Prefect raised his hand, demanding attention.

"Tell me about his influence on other patients?" he asked Gronovski.

"Me? I don't know. He wasn't sayin' much...just looked everyone in the eye."

"How did you feel when he looked at you?"

"I don't know, weird, like..."

"Like what?"

"Like I did something bad...like I needed to confess something."

"Did you?"

"Of course not, Hegemon... I'm not stupid."

"What happened then?"

"Then...then he asked the guards to take him to Johnny."

"Who?"

"Him." Gronovski pointed at the churchman. "The FTC leader was taking a rehabilitation course with us in a high-security cell."

"Did the guards fulfill the defendant's request?"

"Yes..." Gronovski hesitated and glanced at the cage.

"See, Hegemon? He stares at me again, saying something with his eyes."

"Continue. What happened next?"

"Nothing. Johnny—Reverend John, got suddenly cured, stopped attacking people…"

"It was a temporary illness, nothing serious," the FTC leader quickly added.

"Yeah, temporary thing…" Gronovski agreed.

"Do you attest that the defendant has healing powers?" Marcus asked.

"Motivational abilities, your Clemency," Johnny the Baptist clarified.

"What's *attest* mean?" Gronovski was confused.

"It means, 'confirm.' "

"Ah, I don't know about that, but the reverend was suddenly okay, so we let him go and let him take this J. C. guy with him—what they call it?—under his responsibility."

"Clarify this. What does it mean?"

"If anything goes wrong, we would take him back."

"You may now sit," the Prefect told Gronovski before turning to Johnny. "The rest we know, as you described it in your deposition. But why did you name the show 'Jesus 2000'?"

"Purely for marketing purposes." Johnny the Baptist shrugged. "It sounded more intriguing, and this was the approximate year when the defendant was born."

"But, this name also has a religious connotation. Were you aware of that?"

"Yes, but only partially. After all, Jesus is a very common name, and without adding 'Christ,' no one could accuse us of stirring up religious propaganda."

"So, it helped the popularity of the show. How profitable was it?"

"Reasonably successful, your Clemency."

"What did you do with the proceeds?"

"The largest portion was never found, regretfully. What was left barely covered our losses associated with the closing of the show."

"Do you suspect that the defendant embezzled these funds?"

"Yes, your Clemency. Just as it is stated in our deposition."

The Prefect eyed J. C.

"I doubt that," he said. "So far, I do not see clear evidence of the crime committed by the defendant. I declare this session adjourned!"

"Good news, they will acquit him!" Lucas said, relieved.

"Really? I can't believe it." Meg beamed.

"You better not," Thomas said gloomily.

"What do you mean?" Lucas asked.

"They will find him guilty. You will see."

CHAPTER 27
NOT GUILTY!

THE NEXT DAY, the crowd besieging the Caesar Colosseum dwindled considerably. The townspeople were frustrated by the lack of action and the apparent intention of the chief justice to acquit the defendant.

"The city mob is thirsty for blood, not witness testimony," Thomas said as they watched the proceedings from under the roof of the Colosseum.

The chief justice and his assistants took their places, and the guards brought in the defendant, who looked around with a lost, timid smile. The secretary called the next witness: the technician who installed the underwater strings for the show.

"What was the purpose of this device?" the Prefect asked.

"The illusion of walking on water, your Clemency."

"And it worked?"

"Like a Swiss clock. No one in the audience suspected anything."

"Who ordered the installation?"

"That I don't know."

"How come? You do not know who gave the order to use this trick to fool the audience?"

The chief technician hesitated.

"Well?"

"No one, your Clemency. The net was already there when I was hired to install it." The technician wiped his balding head with a handkerchief.

"It's so obvious that this man is lying like everyone else," Meg said. "Terrible city, terrible people…"

"This court doesn't even allow a lawyer to provide at least some kind of a defense," Lucas observed.

"There were no formal attorneys in ancient Rome either," Thomas noted. "Don't forget, these people are trying to copy it."

"So did the Nazis," Lucas said. "And we know how that ended. But here, no lawyer is needed to see that the defendant has nothing to do with the fraud. He is the real victim."

"And yet, he will be found guilty at the conclusion of the trial," Thomas said.

"You speak about it so…calmly." Meg shivered. "Don't you feel sorry for Him?"

"Don't get upset, my child." The old man calmed her. "Of course I sympathize with Him, despite not even knowing who He is, but I do know these people—what they have become."

"It's so…sad."

"Sad, indeed, but true. The Great Crash destroyed many lives…and souls."

The trial continued, and on the third day, even fewer spectators came to the Colosseum. Lucas, Meg, and Thomas were alone on the upper tier of the balcony, but as soon as they took their seats, they felt the tension. Something important was being prepared, something that would decide the fate of the defendant. They watched as a special SS unit in black coats encircled the arena, and a group of workers brought out a large flat basin, connected a hose, and began to fill it with water. A giant man in an SS uniform entered the arena, unlocked the cage, and led the defendant to the edge of the basin.

"Who is this ogre?" Meg whispered in horror.

"First Centurion Goliath—the maniac who killed scores of people, including his own family," Thomas said. "His presence is a very bad sign."

The Centurion pushed J. C. to the steps leading into the basin and paused, awaiting the command. Prefect Marcus gazed at the water, then at the defendant, and signaled with his hand. The Centurion swung his arm, shoving the accused into the basin as the lights went out and darkness filled the Colosseum.

"Lights! Turn on the light!" the audience screamed.

After a long minute, the lights slowly came to life, illuminating frightened faces in the stands, the arena, the basin, and the defendant who stood motionless—on the surface of the water.

"What the…" Lucas uttered, totally confused. "It's impossible! It's some kind of hoax again."

"Believe it, believe it—this is not a hoax," Meg assured him.

"I need to touch this J. C. and the water under his feet myself before I believe it," Thomas said, shaking his head. "It could be a high-tech hologram."

J. C. looked around helplessly, astounded by his transformation. He shifted his eyes down to where his feet barely touched the water and froze, unable to move. It seemed that he was even more amazed at what had happened than anyone else. Yet, his thin figure in a shabby prison jacket made him look miserable.

"So much for the Messiah," Thomas said.

"He *is* the Messiah! I don't understand how you all cannot see it," Meg said.

"I don't believe in *seeing is believing*. I prefer *touching is believing*." Thomas shrugged.

"How can you be so...so cruel?" Meg's eyes darkened with anger.

"Please, you both—stop it," Lucas said. "It is what it is. We have to accept it, although I don't understand what's going on, myself."

The Prefect left the podium, went down to the arena, and approached the basin. He stared closely at the defendant, took a dagger from the guard, dipped its blade into the water, and moved it twice under the feet of the accused, left and right, to make sure that he really stood on the surface without any support. The Prefect's face did not change when he saw the result. He returned to his place, turned to the crowd, and raised his hand in a Julius Caesar gesture. Deathly silence blanketed the entire Colosseum as the crowd awaited his decision.

"People of Vega City, I announce my verdict!" the Prefect said in a loud, commanding voice. *"Not guilty!"*

The crowd roared its disapproval.

"Bravo!" Meg clapped her hands.

Marcus continued to hold his hand up, demanding silence.

"I declare the defendant not guilty of fraud and grand theft." The Prefect paused. "However, in the light of new evidence uncovered during the trial, the accused must remain in custody pending the completion of additional investigative steps."

"What? They won't let him go?" Meg fell in her chair in despair.

"Meg, please, you're taking it too personally," Lucas said. "He still has a chance. We all have a chance!"

"Regretfully, I was right," Thomas said as the court session ended. They were making their way through the throng. Lucas was gloomy, trying to absorb what had just happened. Meg walked behind, swallowing her tears.

The clear evening skies darkened, and electric discharges flashed inside the clouds that loomed over the city.

"The storm is coming," Thomas said, lifting his wrinkled face to the first drops of rain. "Strange, I haven't seen a thunderstorm here for years."

"It's a sign," Lucas said softly.

"Maybe, maybe not," Thomas objected. "One thing is clear —nothing good will come out of it."

"You mean the thunderstorm?"

"I mean the trial."

CHAPTER 28
NIGHT DELIBERATION

MARCUS, Prefect of California and Nevada, walked into the upper colonnade of the Caesar Palace adjacent to the Colosseum. The recent thunderstorm had passed through the city, illuminating the dark horizon with silent shimmering light on its way to the ocean. The flames in Roman cressets on bronze tripods bubbled in the night wind, casting shadows from the palm trees on God's Garden. Marcus could not sleep that night. What had happened? Did he expect it? The answer to the last question was "yes," as odd as it may sound. Somehow, after barely glancing at the suspect for the first time, he knew that J. C. was not an ordinary man. His long hair, the rags he was dressed in, even his penetrating stare had little to do with it. What was striking to the Prefect had been hidden in the suspect's whole being—something troubling, even frightening. The Prefect realized that accusations of fraud against J. C. were shaky, but he could not ignore them because the people demanded justice, and word of the trial had already reached SS headquarters in California. Marcus unfolded the dispatch he had just received: It was the Supreme Council reminding him that the SS movement aimed at preserving the safety of the planet was fighting the spread of religious cults that proclaimed the dominant role of

God, leading society away from the path of social reforms and justice.

Breathing the night air and gazing at the moon rising from the light clouds, Marcus thought about his long career. Born and raised in California, he had never faced the question of what side of the political spectrum he belonged to. The Progressive Party was his natural choice. Forty years ago, California became what was then called a "blue" state, controlled by "progressive" forces, i.e. Democrats, liberals, socialists, etc. There was no political future for anyone who lived in California at the time, but to become a member of the Progressive Party, the umbrella organization for all of these groups. Marcus remembered that idealistic era, how he, young and energetic, joined other supporters of freedom, democracy and equality. He promptly advanced through party ranks—until the crisis of 2029. The country suddenly became torn apart by extremist groups within all major political movements. The Devils of Democracy or D.D. advocated freedom and emancipation in everything—from the choice of gender by children without parental control and the legalization of the most extreme sexual preferences – to the abolition of the family and the forced re-education of all conservatives and churchgoers.

On the opposite side of the state's political spectrum was the Conservative Cataclysm or C.C., which attempted to prevent what they called the moral degradation of society by bringing the country back to its early postcolonial roots, where women essentially had no civil rights and any sexual experimentation in one's bedroom was often punishable by death. Conservative Cataclysm supporters accused their Democratic opponents of an attempt to eliminate the very concept of gender in order to reduce the world population for the benefit of the global elite.

As a result, more moderate conservatives and some progressives formed an alternative—the Security Servants movement. It attracted many, including Marcus, because at the initial stage it advocated restoring public order to prevent social and political chaos that could lead to the country's self-destruction.

This included the fight against religious cults, which since the year 2000 had heralded the approach of the End of the World, stirring panic among the population.

The Prefect was lost in his thoughts. He looked at the city below, flooded with moonlight. What was the will of the people? It was obvious—they all demanded a clear-cut reso-lution, not half-hearted measures. He could not help but notice the reaction of his own soldiers to the defendant's acquittal. The SS guards were disappointed, and the public was outraged. They all needed someone to blame for their suffering. He must continue the trial, allowing people to pour out all of their grievances.

"Guards!" the Prefect shouted in a commanding voice. "Bring Centurion Goliath to me!"

CHAPTER 29
GUILTY OF ALL
MORTAL SINS

DAYS PASSED, but no news came from the Caesar Palace. The people waited for the court to resume the hearings, and every day, the frustration grew.

"Do it, and be done with it!" the public chanted on the streets.

Against all odds, Lucas and Meg still hoped that justice would finally prevail and the Messiah would be set free.

The seventh day of the trial started with the announcement that the High Court would resume the hearings. More troops surrounded the Colosseum as the crowd of spectators poured in. It was a strange and sinister scene with thousands of lost, angry faces illuminated by flaming torches.

"What happened to the electricity?" Lucas wondered.

"I think they turned it off to emphasize the importance of what is about to happen," Thomas said. "Nothing good though."

"What if a fire starts?" Meg asked.

"I guess we all have to die." Thomas cracked a smile.

The air inside was hot and stuffy.

"I've never seen these many unhappy faces in one place!" Lucas said, peering into the crowd. "Look down there—those people next to the arena."

"Those are witnesses for the prosecution," Thomas said.

Lucas studied their faces, and one of them especially struck him: an old woman dressed in black. It appeared that her face was once attractive but had become deathly frozen. She stared at the world through blind eyes as she leaned forward, shaking her head and talking to herself.

What grief must have struck her that she has lost her mind? Lucas thought.

"I declare the court session open!" the Prefect announced as the guards brought in the accused. The Messiah seemed even more miserable than before. He avoided looking at the people around Him, instead directing His gaze inward as if He was listening to the voice inside of Him.

"Secretary, read the statement," Marcus said.

The court secretary came to the front.

"The people of Vega City accuse the defendant of new charges. These allegations include but are not limited to murder, attempted murder, rape, child molestation, war crimes, mass executions..." The prosecution list was long and terrifying.

"What? What's this supposed to mean?" Lucas said as they all froze in surprise."Am I dreaming, is it a joke, or have they all gone mad?

"They are very serious, I am afraid," Thomas said. "I feared something like this would happen."

"What? Please tell us." Lucas turned to him.

"I will tell you in a minute. Just wait a bit more."

"How do you plead? Guilty or not guilty?" the Prefect said.

"I...I don't know," said J. C., barely audible.

"You do not know if you committed these crimes?"

"I don't understand what I am accused of." J. C. lifted his eyes, fixing them on the chief justice.

"The charges against you are based on the testimony of

witnesses. Currently, there are seven hundred and fourteen of them, and many more may follow."

"I…don't understand."

"You mean you don't see what you have to do with it?"

"Yes."

"It will become apparent to you in the course of these hearings," The Prefect said. "In the meantime, the secretary will record your plea as *not guilty*."

The Prefect turned to the secretary. "Call the first witness."

"The court asks Iliad White to take the witness stand," the secretary said.

The woman in black raised her head and strode into the arena, holding the hand of a younger woman, obviously her guide.

"State your name," the Prefect said.

"Iliad White."

"Your age?"

"Twenty-nine."

The audience in the hall rustled in surprise.

"She is lying; she can't be twenty-nine," Meg said indignantly.

"Tell us your story."

Iliad's bloodless lips moved as she gathered her strength to speak.

"I…my husband and I were desperate to have a baby, but it took almost ten years until our little Bobby was born. We nearly lost our minds with happiness when he smiled, seeing our faces. Bobby was strong and healthy. He was God's creation, I thought, and God had sent us this precious gift."

"What happened then?"

"I…I can't…"

"You must. You are the key witness for the prosecution."

A pregnant pause followed, interrupted only by the witness's sobbing.

"Well?"

"My son died when he was only five months old."

"How did it happen?"

"I took him in a baby stroller for a walk. It was a sunny day, and there were other children in the playground too. I began talking to their parents, but when I looked back, Bobby was gone! The stroller was empty. I asked the other parents for help, and together we searched the area but couldn't find Bobby. Then…then my husband came with the police. We looked everywhere all day and all night. I hoped that Bobby was hiding somewhere and we would find him. I still hope and pray for it."

The Colosseum was silent as people listened to the mother's dramatic testimony. Meg was swallowing her tears. The defendant in the cage bowed his head and closed his eyes.

"Continue with your testimony," the Prefect addressed the witness.

"Police stopped the search, but I couldn't. My Bobby was out there somewhere, calling for me. I heard his little voice…"

"What happened then?"

"I found my son's body in an abandoned garage. Raped and stabbed."

The hall froze as the last words settled in people's minds. Meg and some of the other women cried.

"Calm down, Meg," Lucas comforted her and gave her a hug. He eyed the audience. *Who would think these people would still be capable of human emotions?* he thought, seeing the crying women and the upset faces of the men.

The hearing resumed after a long pause when the witness was allowed to speak.

"The light went out of my eyes, and I turned blind that day…but the police didn't believe me. They demanded my confession. They said I killed my son and faked my blindness. Explaining my grief and how I felt to them was impossible, and I began losing my mind. I stopped recognizing people, and my husband left me—he'd had enough, he said—and then, they sent me to a mental hospital."

"How long did you stay there?"

"I don't remember—long, until it was closed. They said the city had no money. I don't remember… I…I don't see anything now. I don't want to see anything!"

"Finish your testimony."

The witness was silent, apparently not hearing the request.

"I am asking you…" the Prefect said slowly, "to complete your testimony. What did you do next?"

"I begged for food out in the streets, telling everybody what happened, and some kind people took me to the Messiah."

"What did the defendant say when he saw you?"

"He just touched my head and said he knows everything and that I should stop tormenting myself."

"Did you believe him?"

"I…thought I did."

"How did you feel?"

"I felt better as if a heavy load had fallen from my chest. But then I thought, *How could God let this happen to Bobby?* If God is real, why do thousands of children die? Then, I thought it must be a false God and a false Messiah!"

"I have no further questions." The Prefect gestured to the guide to lead the witness away, but Iliad did not move. She turned her blind eyes to the cage, listening.

"Poor woman," J. C. said quietly from the cage, as if the wind had blown away. "I have no power to save you, but your child is saved and looks at you from heaven."

"What's going on?" Marcus glared at the cage and waved to the guards. "Get her out at once!"

Soldiers grabbed Iliad and took her from the stage.

"Messiah, Messiah! Glory to you, Son of God!" the blind woman suddenly exclaimed. Her face brightened, as if the past that tormented her had temporarily gone away.

The Colosseum crowd went amok. Some shouted insults, some praised the Lord, and some demanded the witness be arrested and prosecuted together with the main suspect.

After order was restored, Marcus signaled the secretary to come closer. "You must better control your witnesses," the Prefect said in a threatening voice. "I will not allow any outbursts of religious propaganda in my court."

"Yes, your Clemency. Forgive me." The secretary shivered in fear.

In the tense silence that followed, the breathing of hundreds of people could be heard.

"Why didn't He restore her sight?" Lucas leaned towards Thomas.

"You cannot restore what a person does not want," the old man sighed.

"Thomas, please, what are they doing?" Lucas confronted the professor. "I think you know, but you don't tell us. It just doesn't make any sense: They tried Him, accusing Him of deceit, but when they saw that He was not a deceiver, they condemned Him for even worse crimes. How's this possible?"

"You still don't see it?" Thomas said. "What we are witnessing here is the prosecution of God's representative, who they hold accountable for failing to protect the population from atrocities and mass killings."

"So, if He is not the Son of God, He is guilty of fraud—but if He is, He is guilty of murder?"

"That's right. In either case, He will be condemned. This way, they will destroy religion, which is their main goal. The New Order demands it."

CHAPTER 30
COMING TO AMERICA

ARCHBISHOP AVANELLA CONDUCTED Sunday Mass in the Church of Saint Philomena near Turin's once-famed street, *Corso Vittorio Emanuele*. The church stood closed for years and was so small that many parishioners referred to it as a chapel. The archbishop had chosen it because, unlike other city churches decorated in gold and marble, the Church of Santa Philomena had plain undecorated walls, a modest altar, and only a few images of forever-young virgins who lived and died as martyrs nearly two thousand years before. This simplicity, the archbishop felt, was more appropriate after the destruction of St. John the Baptist Cathedral.

Only a few people attended the morning service. Savorelli was one; the other rare guest was Inspector Frescatto. Their faces in the weak morning light were sad, tired, and depressed. All felt that the loss of the Holy Shroud deprived the city of something very important, something that constituted its spirit.

At the end of the Mass as parishioners were approaching the altar for the archbishop's blessing, he asked Savorelli and Frescatto to join him for a walk to the cathedral's ruins. It was still early morning and the streets were empty as they headed towards *Piazza San Giovanni*. In silence, they took *Via Giovanni*

Batista Viotti, and although they walked the same street, in their thoughts, all three parted ways. Monsignor Avanella suddenly realized that the main reason he had chosen the Church of Saint Philomena was probably not its simplicity and low-key appearance. It was much more than that. This saint was the protector of infants, babies, and the youth. He subconsciously linked her tragic fate to the story of the Holy Shroud —from St. Philomena's early death as a virgin martyr to total obscurity and from recognition as a saint back to non-recognition after the Holy See ordered that her name be removed from all liturgical calendars in 1961. A similar fate haunted the Holy Shroud. The Relic was lost over the centuries, recovered in 1354, and acquired wide recognition— only to be questioned as a medieval forgery after a radio-carbon test. Hundreds of miracles on Saint Philomena's grave and the healing of believers in Turin hardly mattered nowadays to iconoclasts. To him, however, it was plain and simple: both Saint Philomena and the Holy Shroud were important parts of his faith. This is how Archbishop Avanella felt deep in his heart.

Seignior Savorelli was far removed from the ephemeral complications of religion. His main concern was how much he should donate this time. He always donated generously when times were good and less when times were bad, but he was rarely present during church services on either occasion. What for? His wife would pass along the latest rumors after each Mass, which she attended every Sunday and every holiday *religiously.* Wasn't this enough? Passing the closed Del Cambio restaurant, Savorelli slowed his steps. *Here it is!* he thought. This was a famous place: beautiful rooms, expensive service, and a divine kitchen out of which came an exquisite mixture of Mediterranean and Northern Italian cuisine. All international stars visiting Turin considered it as a must to dine here at least once. And look at it now: doors blocked permanently with plywood, windows blinded with graffiti-covered shutters, and trash piled up on the sidewalk in front of it. This was a lesson to be learned: Don't grow too big or you risk repeating the fate of all fancy big restaurants in this city that had died out like the dinosaurs. Meanwhile, Savorelli managed to survive...for now. But, what if Monsignor Avanella asks him for a big donation—point-blank, right in front of the charred building of their beloved cathedral? He couldn't say no to the Church, which was like home to him, yet any large donation now would kill him and his business. He simply wouldn't survive.

Inspector Frescatto was also uneasy about their trip. What if the archbishop asks him about the results of his investigation right in front of the cathedral, which would be like being in the presence of a victim's body, still warm after a murder? How would Frescatto confess that after almost two months of investigations, he had found absolutely nothing? He still had no clue regarding the whereabouts of the perpetrators or the purpose of their theft. He expected a ransom note, which had happened in their city before, but no one had contacted police, church, or city authorities. What would he tell the archbishop—that the city police force had no force except an elderly secretary and two part-time officers? That his department had only two old bicycles as means of transportation? The archbishop and the municipality needed the Relic, not his excuses. Ashamed, Frescatto turned away, trying to hide his feelings.

They stopped in front of the charred remains of the cathedral. At first, all three stood there, unable to say a word. Frescatto could almost hear the seconds of this silence tick away before Archbishop Avanella finally broke it. "I have called upon you to advise me what course of action we should choose to resurrect these ruins."

His listeners exhaled with relief. To give advice was easy. Inspector Frescatto spoke first. "We must remove all debris, and I will personally search for clues that may still be there."

"I think we need to fix the roof first because rain will destroy everything that's left in there," Savorelli suggested. "It would be good to cover the windows, at least with plastic, so the building would be preserved for future work. I am ready to donate my services and will provide food to the workers—not much though."

The archbishop put his hands on their shoulders.

"You are both right. We will install a new roof and new stained-glass windows, but first and foremost, the cathedral must be cleaned thoroughly—inside and out. Our entire church should become the Church of Redemption. Together with other religious denominations, we must restore our faith, our belief in God. After all, we as clergy must bear our portion of responsibility for what happened, not only here in this cathedral but in the entire world that has come to its present state." The archbishop's eyes were shining.

Savorelli cleared his throat. "Well, whatever you say, Monsignor. I'm in." He turned to Frescatto. "What about you, chief?"

Totally confused, the inspector nodded.

"The police are with us, Monsignor," Savorelli reported to the archbishop.

"*Ispettore, ispetorre! Monsignor!*"

A police officer from Frescatto's office rode over to them on a police bicycle. "Important news!" the officer exhaled, catching his breath.

"Well, shoot!" the inspector said, still trying to figure out what the archbishop had just told them. *What did he mean about taking responsibility for what the world had become?* As far as Frescatto was concerned, he and his department had done nothing wrong carrying out their duties as best as they could under the circumstances. So, did the Church provide moral guidance? And, how were they responsible for the collapse of the global economy?

"What happened?" asked the archbishop. "Take a deep breath, and tell us in a clear voice."

"*Scusa signore.*" The officer turned to the archbishop. "I am very excited."

"I see it."

"Giovanni Amato."

"What about the poor man? He died?"

"He…woke up."

"You mean, he came out of a coma?"

The officer nodded.

Everyone froze in disbelief.

"Give me your bicycle," the archbishop said, looking at his companions. "See you all there."

The convoluted passages inside Turin's city hospital seemed endless as Avanella rushed to the intensive care unit. His loud steps echoed through the building. A nun in a black cassock met him at the entrance of Giovanni's room.

"The patient is very weak, Monsignor, so please be considerate," the nun said, leading the archbishop to Giovanni's bed.

Avanella slowly bent down to the watchman.

"Giovanni, my friend, can you hear me?"

The watchman's barely audible breath became more rapid as he opened his eyes. A ghost of a smile appeared on his pale lips. With great effort, he moved his hand and gestured for the archbishop to get closer.

"Don't strain yourself too much," said Avanella, seeing the watchman's efforts. "Doctors say you need rest. You can tell me everything later."

The watchman slowly shook his head.

"L…Luca…"

"I am sorry, Giovanni, your son is not here," the archbishop said softly. "Lucas is far away, very far."

The watchman shook his head one more time. "Luca and...*He*...*He* is in danger."

"Who are you talking about, Giovanni? Who is 'He'?"

Old Giovanni closed his eyes, lying still.

"Please, Monsignor, you must leave," the nun implored.

"Just one more minute, *por favor*." Avanella put his ear to the old man's mouth, listening.

"Messiah..." gasped the old man.

When Inspector Frescatto and Savorelli entered the ward, they saw Giovanni and the archbishop near the watchman's bed, praying.

"Giovanni, how are you?" Savorelli said loudly.

Avanell waved him away, signaling the restaurateur to be silent. He motioned for the other visitors to leave and remained alone, mentally saying goodbye to his friend.

The two men waited in front of the hospital, not knowing what to do. Should they stay here, or did the monsignor want them to return home?

"Don't you think the archbishop acts strange lately?" Savorelli asked his partner.

"What do you mean?" Irritated, the inspector glanced at his noisy companion.

"I say the monsignor is not the same after the fire. He wears no red cassock and no hat anymore, not even during Mass."

"The fire and the theft affected all of us, in case you hadn't noticed, Savorelli."

"I understand, I'm just saying it's strange." The restaurateur sighted. "How long do we have to wait here?"

"As long as needed."

The clock on *Piazza San Carlo* chimed three times as the archbishop stepped out of the building. His gaze was distant as if it was directed somewhere far away. He passed the two men and headed back to his office.

"How is Giovanni, Monsignor? Is he feeling better?" asked Savorelli, who had followed him.

"He passed away."

"*Oh, Signore!*"

"Rest his soul, Lord!" said the inspector, who had joined them. "Did he say who the thieves were and why he burned down the cathedral?"

Avanella stopped and eyed the two men.

"He said much more, my friends. Get ready, we are going to America."

CHAPTER 31
SAILING AWAY

THE NEWS that Archbishop Avanella was gathering a group of believers to join him in his journey spread through the city. Thousands volunteered, but only twenty were chosen. But, even these people hardly knew what the purpose of the trip would be. Because even monthly flights to America had ended, no one had a clue how they would all get there either. Archbishop Avanella scrambled to find the solution as he did not have much time. The last words of Giovanni Amato stuck in his mind: Lucas was in danger, and so was someone whom the deceased called the Messiah. There was something else that deeply disturbed the archbishop, something the watchman said in Latin right before his death. Although the phrase was lost in a death rattle, the archbishop was positive that it began with *"Descensus…"* What was it? Avanella hoped to find the answer across the ocean.

Facing the problem of how to get there, the archbishop developed a plan. Instead of a plane, they would travel by boat. Fishermen were still sailing along the coast, and all he needed was to find a ship large enough to carry them to New Amsterdam. The best place to start the search was Venice where his friend Bishop Francis lived. A former fisherman, the bishop was a patron of the seamen and their families who turned to him for all of their spiritual needs. Avanella wrote him a letter but received no response. He wasn't surprised; hardly anyone trusted the domestic postal service. This had been a well-known issue for decades, which only worsened after the Great Crash. To reach his friend, Avanella would have to travel by train. Old steam engines were still in use, and they didn't require fancy electrical grids or diesel fuel.

The locomotive FS 740 pulled a few battered cars to the brick-and-stone causeway *Ponte della Liberta*, which crossed the Venetian lagoon. Expecting to exit at Santa Lucia station as he had done many times before, the archbishop was stunned to see the last-century station building flooded up to the rail tracks. Passengers were jumping on wooden planks, making their way out to the makeshift pier where ferry boats of all sizes and shapes were tied to massive wooden poles. Reaching the pier, Avanella froze in place because of the unpleasant surprise. The unfamiliar city stood in front of him like a wounded warrior waist-deep in water. The streets were gone and so were many bridges; the crosses on the city's towers were slanted, and shutters blinded the churches' stained-glass windows. This was all the result of rising sea levels. The archbishop gasped and muttered a short prayer.

"Hey, are you going to stand there or jump into my gondola?" A tall ferryman with a weathered face held out his hand.

"Oh, *me scusi padre*," he said, seeing a white tab collar on the archbishop's clergy shirt. "Let me help you, padre, with your suitcase."

They sailed through a maze of narrow canals that were once city streets. The lower levels of the buildings had disappeared under the waters of the lagoon, and the windows above them were turned into front doors with makeshift piers in front.

"These homes won't last long," the ferryman said. "You see their brick walls? The water reached all the way up, far above the safe level of the waterproof white stone base. This is the end."

Avanella said nothing. It was painfully clear to him that his beloved city, where he studied and spent a large portion of his life, was dying and would soon disappear in the blue waters of the Mediterranean.

The marble octagonal walls of Basilica di Santa Maria della Salute or *La Salute*, as the locals called it, rose from the waters of the Grand Canal. Miraculously, the sea stopped at the last step of the white stone staircase leading to the cathedral. The front gates were open, and it seemed their gondola was about to sail right inside.

Avanella found his friend alone at the main altar, praying in front of Saint Mary's mosaic image.

"Peace to you, Bishop, and your city." Avanella kneeled beside his friend. Francis turned to his voice and smiled joyfully. "What a pleasant surprise!"

"What happened to your bishop's maroon shirt?" Francis added, standing up and embracing his friend. "You're not a priest anymore."

"Correct, I still find it hard to believe." Avanella chuckled. "Just like you, Bishop. We are both yesterday's priests. It would only be possible in the early Church when Christianity just started its history. I guess the Church now begins its journey all over again."

"Maybe…right after the Great Flooding," Francis said, looking around. "Sorry, bad joke."

"And you, Bishop, are busy praying and feeding your flock."

"Praying, my dear Avanella, praying. That's all I can do.

Let us not forget Venice's deliverance from the pestilence when this church was built in the seventeenth century."

"Yes, of course, the bubonic plague. Many believed St. Mary saved the city."

"Who else? Definitely not the magistrate. Now we need divine protection like never before."

"I agree." They both fell silent.

Bishop Francis raised his head, driving away gloomy thoughts. "Forgive me, my friend. I'm keeping you here, and you are probably hungry after the trip. How long did it take you to get here? A week...or two, perhaps?" Both chuckled.

The light of the fireplace reflected in their wine glasses as they were finishing their meal—a few slices of pecorino toscano cheese, local fish, and white peaches. Bishop Francis was pensive, staring at the fire. "What a sad story. I heard of the disaster—the theft and the destruction of the cathedral, but I didn't know the details."

"Do you think you can help me to get to the States? Maybe one of the fishermen could lend me a boat?"

"Well, about the sailing boat. You won't find any that are decent and large enough. The fishing boats here were all used to the limit without repair. Sorry." He paused. "But I may still be able to help you out with your adventure. Did you see this?" Francis pulled out a picture from a pile of books on a side table.

Avanella studied the futuristic lines of a catamaran yacht in the photo. He shrugged. "I'm not a millionaire. Who in his right mind would let me use it?"

"It's a long story. It is supposed to be the most advanced zero-emission, carbon-neutral, or whatever yacht in the world —sort of an advanced version of the one that brought the child ecology crusader, Greta Walz, to the UN General Assembly in New Amsterdam."

"Yes, I remember," Avanella said. "Continue, please."

"A shady billionaire built it for P.R. purposes and asked the Church to bless it. But then came the Great Crash. He lost his fortune and shot himself or was shot by his creditors. Who knows."

"And?"

"La Vagabonde 0 is still docked in an abandoned pier on Lido Island, collecting port fines. Our authorities are very good at that. All her electronics were stolen, but the helm and her sails are in good shape, and so is her super-composite hull, which is ten times stronger than steel."

"You didn't answer my question, dear Francis. Who would let me use this beauty, let alone cross the ocean in it?" Avanella asked. "You are dreaming, I'm afraid."

Francis's eyes gleamed. "Leave it to me. I didn't provide my services to this city for twenty-four years for nothing. I have my ways."

"How many people—crew and passengers—can it take?"

"How many do you need?"

"Twenty."

"Make it twenty-one."

Avanella smiled, seeing that his friend was still an Italian —he needed to negotiate no matter what. The archbishop accepted the rules of the game.

"Why's that, Francis?" he asked, playing along with his friend.

"Do you think I will let you sail alone? Without a VIP passenger?"

"Who might this passenger be?"

"The one who knows how to sail—a navigator." Francis pointed at himself.

"What will I get for this?"

"My blessing."

Both looked at each other…and laughed.

CHAPTER 32
VENTURING INTO DISASTER

THE TRIAL at the Colosseum continued, and more witnesses for the prosecution came to the stand. Heartrending stories of unimaginable cruelties, war crimes, and the torture of women and children followed one after another. Meg was unable to hold back her tears, while Lucas tried to predict how this mockery, which had little to do with real court proceedings, would end.

"The instinct of procreation and the fear of death rule this world," Thomas explained. "And now the SS wants to prove that these instincts—created by God—lead to terrible crimes, so God is responsible for them!"

"So, these people are preparing to execute the Messiah and God in one person?" Lucas asked.

"Yes, in a way."

Staring at the SS guards and crimson flags with their Nazi-Roman symols. Lucas couldn't help but ask himself what he and his friends could do to change this tragic course of events, which would otherwise come to a very bad end. Meg believed that He was the true Messiah, but was he Jesus 2000 as the name of his show suggested? And, where are those he has healed? Definitely not in this place, filled with pain and hatred.

Lucas turned to his friends. "I must find them."

"Who?" Thomas eyed him.

"Them…all those healed by the Messiah."

"What for? You wouldn't be able to bring them here. This is a one-way street—no defense allowed."

"Thomas, you speak so calmly about it," Meg said.

"I speak the truth, the sad truth. This city and the SS are about to condemn him. The only question is, what form of execution will they choose?"

"But why?" Meg's eyes were filled with pain. "He is not responsible for these crimes. He came to save these people, to heal their wounds!"

"So true," Thomas said. "Actually, I'm not quite sure about it. I must see their healed limbs, touch them to believe. But, the most important thing is that for them [he pointed at the spectators], it is more important to blame someone for their suffering, to place the blame on one man. That's what they all want."

"I'll find those who he had cured," Lucas said.

"I wouldn't recommend it," the old professor remarked. "It can be risky. You will most likely find them outside, but to get back into the crowd would be unwise after your encounter with these individuals."

Meg stood up. "I'll go with you."

"No, please stay." Lucas took her gently by the hand. "I feel better when you're here. I'll be quick."

"Well, then it's probably me who needs to accompany you," Thomas grumbled, getting up from his chair. "I don't know how I can help, but two men are better than one."

"Thank you, Thomas, thank you so much, but I need you both here. You are my eyes and ears."

The former professor gave Lucas a doubtful look. "Something tells me that you are not quite sincere, young man. What are you really up to?"

"I ask you, please—stay here," Lucas said, and their eyes met.

"Well, you are the boss," Thomas said, raising both hands. "Just be careful."

CHAPTER 33

DETAINED

THE CROWD OUTSIDE doubled in size as the trial approached its long-anticipated conclusion. The city folks were everywhere—in the Sports Pavilion, clustered outside the Colosseum entrance gate, and out on the street in front of the building. Their mood was even more hostile than before—towards the accused, the judges, and each other.

"These stupid judges are dragging their feet. What for? He's guilty as hell! Everyone sees it."

"Yeah, to hell with him!"

"Just kill the bastard just like he killed so many innocent people."

"Send this pervert to hell!"

"Hey, you, Four-Eyed, you stepped on my foot. Can't you see where you're going?" someone said, pushing a man in a hat and dark glasses away.

"I'm blind."

"Blind? Then stay at home, idiot. You won't see shit anyway." A few people laughed, pointing fingers at the blind man. "What a knucklehead! Just look at him!"

Lucas approached the man. "Excuse me, let me help you…here." He led the blind man to the wall bordering the street. "You can sit now."

"Bless you, stranger," the man muttered. "What is your name?"

"Lucas."

"Who?"

"Lucas."

"Luke?"

"Well...yes, Luke, if you will."

What a strange man, Lucas thought.

"What are you doing here?" said the stranger.

*How interesting that he is asking **me** what I am doing here,* Lucas wondered. "Well, I am looking for someone—the girl who was recently resurrected, as I heard, and also...other people who were healed," he said.

"By *Him*?"

Lucas eyed the strange man. What was his age? It was impossible to say. The gray hair under his hat was pulled up in a ponytail, and his wrinkled face was as eternal as the mountains of Tibet.

"Yes."

"You won't find these people here."

"How do you know?" Lucas peered into the man's face. Was he really blind?

"Excuse me, you are not blind, are you?"

"Maybe I am. It depends..." The man chuckled. "My name is Maharish. Tell me why you need to see them, and I'll see if I can help."

"You said 'see'?"

"A figure of speech, obviously." Behind his sunglasses, Maharish seemed to look directly at Lucas.

"Yeah, of course." Lucas paused. Why would he tell everything to this "blind" man he had just met?

"I need to see them because they are living proof that He is the real Messiah who came to save the world, not to destroy it."

Maharish quickly checked if anyone could hear their

conversation and removed his shades. He looked at Lucas doubtfully. Was he worthy of his trust?

"I happen to know where to find many of those sufferers who were cured by Him," Maharish said. "These unfortunate souls are hiding in an abandoned planetarium, which they turned into a house of prayer. Are you planning to disclose their location?"

"You know very well that is not my intention." Lucas met Maharish's stare.

"Well, then I will show you where to find them."

"What about the girl? Do you know who she is?"

"Her name is Hope. Her mission is to save Him."

"I don't follow... How could the girl save the Messiah?"

A long pause followed as Maharish hesitated before answering.

"I gave her something for safekeeping—something very important that has inexplicable power," Maharish whispered. "This is a transition to another world. I have no explanation..."

"Hey! This is that bastard who threatened us with the gun!" someone yelled in the crowd. "He beat old Pedro."

"Get him! Kick his ass!"

An angry mob led by the fat woman surrounded Lucas. A tall man leapt forward, aiming his fist at Lucas's face, but Lucas dodged the blow and answered it with his own, sending the man back into the crowd. Knowing that this time he would not be able to fool them with his pager, Lucas turned around, searching for a way to escape. But, someone grabbed him from behind. Lucas blocked the attacker's arm with both hands and threw him over his shoulder to the ground. The mob cursed and hissed, but no one dared to attack him again. Meanwhile, his strange interlocutor vanished behind the violent faces.

"Back off! Back off, I said!" An SS guard made his way through the crowd, followed by two more.

"Your papers!" the guard demanded.

"This was a misunderstanding, officer," Lucas said, taking out his passport. "Here… I'm a tourist."

"Shut up!" The guard studied the document.

"A foreigner? Recently admitted to the country—a security risk." He put the passport in his pocket. "Come with me."

Before Lucas realized what was going on, another guard snapped handcuffs on his wrists, and the soldiers took him away, pushing back the angry crowd.

CHAPTER 34
CONCENTRATION CAMP

THE ARRESTED suspects filled a makeshift concentration camp located in an airport building, and there was little room for a new batch of detainees. Unlike the work of the police at their detention center before, the SS were swift and efficient. Teams of investigators, divided into three officers each, quickly filtered the "human material" into major categories and processed them quickly without courts or lengthy inquiries. Murder suspects and violent criminals were hand-cuffed, blindfolded, and marched to a canyon near the city where firing squads pushed them off cliffs, saving them bullets. The others, mostly petty thieves and prostitutes, were sentenced to stoning but then pardoned and sent to hard labor. The death sentence still hung over them, and there was no job they would refuse, even murder if necessary. In the eyes of SS leaders, Vega City was on the road to recovery as a city of the New Order in which social justice imposed on the population played a supreme role.

Lucas did not fit any of the usual categories, but the SS labeled him a "terrorist suspect," possibly an "anarchist," like the extremists who terrorized America at the beginning of the XXth century. They had played a significant role in committing politically motivated violence: bombings, riots, and killings, including the assassination of president William McKinley, who died as a result of an anarchist bullet in 1901. The federal government responded to the terror with its own —arresting, torturing, and killing suspected terrorists, often without proper proceedings or even clear evidence of a crime.

Now, a century later, the new authorities adopted similar practices, as Lucas quickly learned. As soon as the guards brought him in, he was stripped, searched, and beaten unconscious. He woke up on a wet cement floor in a small room, dimly lit by a tiny energy-saving bulb. He turned his head and found his bloody clothes on the floor, making him realize that he was naked. Clenching his teeth and overcoming pain, Lucas pulled on his jeans and T-shirt. *Why am I doing it?* he wondered. *They will shoot me anyway.* Did he fear death? He couldn't say. All he knew was that he was dead tired. His eyes closed, and he sank back into unconsciousness.

CHAPTER 35
STORM

THE TWO BISHOPS began their transatlantic voyage early in the morning, sailing from the port of Genoa, where they collected a crew of twenty volunteers. Savorelli and Frescatto were among them. As always, the two men were inseparable and, as always, they argued about everything, particularly their personal reasons for taking part in the adventure. Savorelli accused the inspector of neglecting his duties and not admitting to the failure of his investigation, while Frescatto suspected his friend of running away from his wife, who otherwise controlled his every step. Their arguments were loud and reverberated around the entire yacht, which Avanella christened the *Santa Maria*. Bishop Francis couldn't stand these two characters, and his friend knew it. Catching Francis's angry puzzled look, Avanella shrugged, hiding his smile. They were precious pieces of his native city, which he had taken with him.

The *Santa Maria* was a marvel of technical progress, which United Europe had managed to achieve while on the brink of collapse. The yacht had two hulls made of vinyl ester with a Divinycell core where the crew quarters were housed. The hull beneath the waterline was solid steel glass should she ever experience a grounding. Overhead, she carried two carbon Axxon masts and a deck with a flying bridge. Her sails were high-tech solar panels, which could turn and change positions to catch the wind through an intricate network of titanium cables. All she needed was an experienced captain. They couldn't find one, and Bishop Francis with his experience as a fisherman tried to fill the gap as best as he could. Avanella was his first mate or spiritual mentor, depending on the situation. It was a joy to both of them to navigate the *Santa Maria* across the waters of the Mediterranean. A gentle tailwind sped them to their destination.

"Listen, Avanella, I just remembered," Francis said, turning to his friend. "Don't you think we should have notified Rome?" This wasn't *exactly* what he meant to say. He had intended to ask how they expected to succeed in their attempt to reach New Amsterdam illegally with only a small crew, only to then face the entire NAC police force. But, he also realized that it was too late to raise his concerns.

"I thought of it." Avanella smiled. "How much help did you get from what used to be called the Holy See? About none?" He paused. "So, I thought it was sufficient to send them a *letter* asking for their blessing."

"Are you serious?" Francis was delighted. "You know damn well they'll never get it, right?"

"It's all in God's hands." Avanella shrugged and looked into his friend's face, reading his thoughts. "As for the second part of your question, I have no answer to it. Although…" He thought for a moment. "Do you remember the Children's Crusade of 1212?"

"What?" Francis was surprised. "You mean that infamous attempt to peacefully convert Muslims to Christianity?"

"The chronicles at the time call it a heroic attempt to cross the Mediterranean to deliver a message of peace to the Muslim world," Avanella said.

"It didn't end too well, Avanella," Francis reminded him. "These kids were sold to slave traders instead."

"Not quite. These stories came up centuries later, while in reality many of these children returned home, and many stayed in Genoa where they obtained new homes."

"Still, their mission failed, didn't it?"

"Yes, but only because the sea failed to part—to let them walk to the Holy Land as they believed."

"Exactly. Beliefs alone are not enough, no matter how strong."

"Yes and no, my friend." Avanella smiled softly. "Aren't the waters parting in front of us, right before our eyes?" He pointed at the yacht's hulls, slashing through the blue waters of the Mediterranean.

Francis was stunned.

"You got me," he said and patted his friend's shoulder. "God willing, we'll find the way to New Amsterdam."

Passing the Rock of Gibraltar, deserted and populated only by wild monkeys, they immediately encountered the stiff Atlantic wind. The tranquil colors of the Mediterranean disappeared behind them, giving way to gray waves. The headwind was getting stronger and soon turned into a forceful gale. The high-tech sails constantly augmented their footage and position, barely able to keep the yacht on course. Bishop Francis looked at them, cursing the whiz kids who invented this marvel of absurdity. He didn't trust these flimsy gadgets and wished he had regular Scottish pine masts and traditional cotton sails enforced with Dacron, capable of withstanding any storm. One thing he had to admit though: this boat with its twin hulls was more stable than any single-hull vessel. It was impossible to topple the catamaran, no matter how big the waves or powerful the wind. Bishop Francis put on his old clipper parka, scanning the horizon. On the other hand, he thought, if—God forbid—they did keel over, they were dead because there was no way the catamaran would bounce back to its safe position as most single-hull yachts do because of their heavy keels, which served as a counterbalance. You win some, you lose some, he thought. Only God can change it. He checked their compass, a traditional one devoid of fancy computer electronics. It kept the course, and as long as the compass functioned, no GPS was needed. He glanced at the horizon again and turned to his friend.

"I don't like those clouds," Francis grumbled, pointing at a dark spot between the ocean and the sky.

"What about it?" Avanella looked in that direction. "Yes, it's a bit darker than other clouds, but what's the difference?"

"It means a storm." Francis reached for his binoculars. "The only question is how bad is it? Call all men on deck, and take the wheel." He left the bridge.

"Okay, take it easy," Avanella said, taking his position at the helm. "You act like a real captain, but you're not."

The northwest wind gained strength; the waves attacked the yacht, striking it with the force of thousands of tons. Holding tight to the railing, Bishop Francis made his way across the deck. The entire deck was covered with solar panels. They generated electricity and could withstand the weight of a human, but would they withstand the full force of a storm? He wasn't sure. Checking the masts, sails, and rigging of the yacht, he kept looking at the horizon. His gloomy predictions came true: Within minutes, the black spot transformed into a dark mass that swallowed the sky and the ocean. It approached quickly. Seeing the ten-meter-high waves, he knew they were doomed. In the old days, the crew would cut the masts and issue a distress call. But, how would someone cut these elastic poles made of reinforced carbon? And what help could they count on in this vast deserted ocean where ships had not been sailing for years?

"Avanella!" Francis ran back to the cockpit. "Batten down the hatches, and lock the crew in the cabins."

"Is it *that* bad?" Avanella took his eyes off the compass.

Francis nodded.

"What about you?"

"My place is here at the helm."

"We can put it on automatic; it has a storm mode."

"I know, but it's too risky not to keep an eye on everything here."

Avanella looked at his friend. "Are you sure?"

"Yes."

"Then, I'm staying with you," Avanella said. "You won't die without me."

They shook hands. They were confident they would weather the storm.

The next hours stretched out into infinity. The tempest pounded the *Santa Maria* from all directions, gusts of wind bent the masts, and jets of rain flooded the cockpit windows. The waves grew in size, reaching the sky, and then—illuminated by lightning strikes, a black wall of water rose in front of the yacht and brought down its thousand-ton weight on them. It plunged the *Santa Maria* into the abyss of water, only to grab it the next moment and throw it high into the sky. She froze in the air, hanging for long seconds, turned upside down, and began to slide back into the ocean...

That's it, it's over, we've capsized and the yacht will go to the bottom. Avanella thought. *Lord, have mercy on us!*

CHAPTER 36
MAHARISH, END OF JOURNEY

WHEN THE YOUNG man he had just met was detained, Maharish couldn't risk exposing himself as he had a more important mission. He retreated into the crowd and watched as the guards took out the arrested, passed the checkpoint in front of the Caesar Colosseum, and led his new acquaintance to the "black crow," an old school bus painted black and used by the SS to transport detainees. It meant only one thing: They were taking him to the concentration camp, where they sorted out small-time offenders from enemies of the New Order. There was nothing Maharish could do to help the young man now. This was sad because he was obviously a decent person. What was his name? Luke? He was searching for Hope, and so was Maharish, because she disappeared after she thwarted the assassination of the Messiah. Where was she hiding? Did she have the Shroud? Although Dr. Crow's instructions said nothing about her, Maharish knew that the resurrected girl was the key to the mystery that began in Bethlehem Hospital.

Maharish had spent forty years of his life following Dr. Crow in his attempts to create the Son of God. Together with his master, he endured failures and the bitterness of defeat until the great moment when the Messiah's transfiguration took place in the desert. It was sad that Dr. Crow didn't live to see this. What would his master say if he knew about his victory? And would he be surprised to learn that his creation was now being judged by the people's court as the world's most dangerous criminal?

Maharish suddenly felt something stuck in his throat. He coughed, trying to clear it, and went on coughing, unable to stop. It was a dry cough that pierced his chest. He was sweating. He knew it wasn't alcohol, even though he abused it daily, trying to blend in with the masses of outcasts who had flooded the streets of the cities after the crisis. As recently as this morning, he had no symptoms of any illness, but now he felt worse every minute. Something was wrong. As a medical professional, he knew it was not a common cold or flu, but what could it be? After a particularly severe coughing attack, he looked at the handkerchief he used to cover his mouth and saw small bloody pieces of his lungs.

Maharish trudged to his hideout. As it became more difficult to breathe with each step, Maharish remembered how ten years ago, the coronavirus pandemic had paralyzed the planet, sending millions to the morgue. This was the first crisis that led up to the Great Crash. Was it returning now in the form of a new, even more devastating pandemic? Maharish snuck into the power plant and climbed into his boiler tank—home sweet home. He lit his lantern, which illuminated the old Holiday Inn mattress on the floor and a small pillow with the fading sign "My other house is in France." He was losing his breath. No, he thought, this was not a coronavirus. It was something much worse. Feeling he would pass out at any moment, Maharish took out a syringe, filled it with a heroin and crack cocaine mix, and injected it into his vein. This substance, known as a "speedball," would give him the strengths to survive the disease. He felt the illness release him and his body levitate to the rusty dome of the boiler tank. It was his spaceship, traveling among the planets. His heartbeat slowed…and slowed…until it stopped.

CHAPTER 37
DR. PORTNOY

LUCAS WOKE up on the floor of his cell, shuddering and coughing up his lungs. His whole body was on fire; his blood was everywhere. *Is this how death comes?* he thought, trying to figure it out.

The metal door swung open, and Goliath thrust his huge head into the cell.

"Who is this prisoner?" the Centurion asked someone behind him.

"Suspected terrorist from Europe," said the tall guard, stepping forward. He looked like a schoolboy next to his superior.

"Was he processed by the prosecution?"

"No, sir. Something is wrong with him; he's coughing and bleeding nonstop."

"Then take him into the infected cell, and wear a gas mask. It may save you a trip to the graveyard."

"Yes, sir."

The guards dragged Lucas down a long passageway into a large room filled with a shifting mass of bodies.

"This is your new home, get used to it," one of the guards said as they pushed Lucas in. The door slammed behind them.

When Lucas opened his eyes, he saw a living hell: hundreds of inmates piled on the floor, by the walls, and on top of each other. Some were moving erratically, trying to free themselves, while others were lying motionlessly —on their way to death. Only a few were able to wander around, making their way between cursing and breathing piles of human flesh. It was clear to Lucas that all of these people were struck by illness. Their eyes were red, and blood flowed from dozens of open mouths as they tried to take one last breath of air. Only one inmate sat calmly amid this bedlam and gazed at the newcomer. He was in his late fifties, bald, and his face was calm, showing no sign of illness. Lucas moved closer to see this unusual person more clearly, but another fit of coughing prevented him from speaking. Lucas dropped on his knees and uttered a few sounds, which drowned in the blood coming from his mouth.

"I see that you don't feel well," the man said, reaching out and shaking hands with Lucas. "My name is Dr. Portnoy."

"L…Luca…s."

"Try not to speak." The doctor checked his pulse. "Um… your heart rate is very rapid, you have a high fever, about 105, and hypertension, I'd say 250 to 140. The worse news is that you contracted KV—the killer virus."

"Any good news for me?" Lucas tried to smile.

"Not really." The doctor looked around the room. "All these unfortunate people are infected by this virus. They will last a day or two and die."

Lucas followed his gaze.

"How do you know? And…why are *you* still alive?"

"You see, you have calmed down and are no longer coughing. That's the good news." The doctor eyed him. "As for myself… Did you hear about Nazareth, what happened there?"

"You mean the city in Northern Israel?"

"Nazareth, Nevada. I lived there, and I saw *everything.* Do you know about the healer and the dead girl?"

For a moment, Lucas forgot about his own condition. "Yes, I remember. That town was destroyed after an accident at a nuclear test site."

"Yes, and the KV pandemic began there. The official name of the virus is H2N2. Its source was fifteen miles from the town in secret federal facilities that were raided by the SS. That led to a chain of events. In a few days, the guards entered Nazareth and killed the last inhabitants who survived the explosion, and soon the virus killed the soldiers. I was away to see a patient, and I'm the only one who stayed alive after the carnage."

"But, aren't you infected with the virus now, like all of them?" Lucas pointed at the rest of the inmates.

"I drank *His* wine…"

"What wine?"

"The wine *He* gave to people."

"So, you saw Him before He came to Vega City?"

The doctor nodded.

"Tell me what happened," Lucas asked him, suppressing another fit of cough.

Dr. Portnoy looked around and fixed his eyes on the cell door, a piece of metal with no peephole.

"I heard the guards. They called you an Italian terrorist."

"I'm not…"

"Doesn't matter. For them you are," Portnoy said. "I know, you traveled here from Europe to find the thieves and the stolen Relic. Are you from the police?"

"No, just a private person, the son of a victim."

"Now, the question is: Do *you* trust *me?* " Portnoy asked.

"I have to. What choice do I have?" Totally exhausted, Lucas was about to collapse on the floor.

"Then let me do a medical examination first." The doctor checked Lucas's face, his tongue, and the color in his eyes.

"Do you need to do it now?"

"I have to." The doc pulled out a sewing needle hidden in a seam in his jacket and pierced his index finger. "Don't move, and close your eyes."

Lucas shut his eyes and felt the doc's finger touch his mouth.

"Now, lick your lips with your tongue. I'm sorry we don't have distilled water here."

Lucas felt an electric shock course through his body.

"Now, sit closer, and listen to what happened in Nazareth…"

CHAPTER 38
THE CURE

BY THE TIME Portnoy finished his story, Lucas felt better. His cough subsided, and pain loosened its grip on his lungs.

"Your chance of survival is considerably higher now." Portnoy chuckled, enjoying Lucas's astonishment. "No need to thank me. I didn't do anything. My blood produces antibodies, blocking virus development. It saved me, and I do hope it will save you." He glanced at the other infected inmates in the room. "Unfortunately, the concentration of the antibodies in my blood is not nearly enough to save them all, let alone the entire city. And, frankly, I wouldn't want to cure some of these individuals, especially the SS."

"But, how can we get out of here? They don't feed these miserable folks. If we don't die from the virus, we all will die of hunger," Lucas said.

"You're absolutely right," the doc agreed. "It wouldn't hurt us to hurry up a little... Let's see. When we die, they will load us into a garbage truck and dump our bodies in Red Canyon. By the way, this is a very beautiful place. I advise you to visit it sometime."

"You're kidding," Lucas muttered. "Is this the right time for it?"

"It helps me think," Portnoy said and paused. "The trick is

to fool the guards tomorrow when they start emptying the cell. No one can survive the virus for more than two days. We can hide among dead bodies, but the Centurion personally checks the dead by piercing them with a bayonet. Did you have a chance to meet this gentleman?"

"I did, unfortunately," Lucas said.

"So, it does seem to be our only chance – to escape by pretending to be dead. Are you prepared to take this risk?"

"We cannot die twice," Lucas said. "I'm ready."

"Then, *alea jacta est*," Portnoy said. "You're Italian; do you know what this Latin phrase means?"

"Yes, point of no return, basically. Julius Caesar said it before crossing the Rubicon River to begin his conquest of Rome."

"I see you feel much better now." Portnoy studied Lucas's face. "The whites of your eyes are still a bit reddish, but the virus will soon be gone. Well, let's get ready."

CHAPTER 39
MISSION IMPOSSIBLE

ARCHBISHOP AVANELLA barely remembered what happened after *Santa Maria* was flipped by gigantic waves. Only one image was imprinted in his memory: water rushing through the door into the cockpit, knocking them down, and the yacht plunging into darkness.

Regaining consciousness, Avanella opened his eyes and looked around. The tail of the storm had passed through, disappearing behind the stern. Oddly enough, the damage caused by the storm was minor. The side door of the cockpit was smashed into pieces, the observation window was cracked, one of the masts was gone, but the yacht was still upright. How was it possible? How did Santa *Maria* return to the safe position after she flipped upside-down in the waves, which presumably meant certain death for all of them? And where was Francis?

"Francis!" Avanella called. Now he remembered how he and everything around him had fallen deeper and deeper into the abyss. If this was not the end, then what was it? What brought them back to the surface? He closed his eyes—darkness, darkness—and then, an overwhelming mass of light caught the yacht and thrust it to the surface. Was it the second wave that pulled them out of the watery grave or something else? *Your faith has saved you,* Avanella remembered the Bible from Luke 7:50.

Now he needed to check if his friends had survived the storm too.

"Francis!" he yelled.

"I'm here—you don't have to scream so loud." Francis climbed the captain's bridge. Although he pretended that nothing had happened, his bruises and a big gash on his forehead said otherwise. Avanella smiled with relief.

"You need to take care of that scratch, it looks pretty nasty." He pointed at Francis's wound.

"Yeah, tell me about it." Bishop Francis checked his reflection in a broken shard of glass and looked back at his friend. "I'm glad you are okay. How did we manage to ride out the storm?"

"I'm asking that myself. What about the crew?"

"I just checked. They did as I told them and locked themselves in the lower cabins, and both hulls served as pantones. They are fine, except those two from Turin. One has a broken arm, and the other a broken nose. I told you it would be better to leave them both at home."

"It's kind of too late now, isn't it?" Avanella said.

Francis examined the yacht's digital GPS system. "Let's see if it still works. *E rotta!* As I expected, the main compass broke down—all integrated circuits are busted. Good thing we also have a magnetic compass, this little *bambino.*" He went to the binnacle, housing a compass in front of the steering wheel.

"You're talking like a fisherman, not a clergyman, Francis," Avanella observed. "Steer the yacht to its destination."

"I know my responsibilities, don't remind me," the bishop grumbled.

He examined the compass. Since his days as a young man, he was fascinated with these ingenious devices, which showed a traveler the right direction to go anywhere on the planet except for blackout zones. Magnetic compasses, called "Kelvin Spheres" after the name of their inventor, incorporated two compensating spheres and were easy to adjust. The one they had was a Ritchie Navy Standard Compass. The storm damaged it too—the glass was cracked, and the electric lights were out—but the floating dial inside of it was intact.

"Good old boy," Francis muttered. "You still need some adjustment, but you will be like new again."

Inspector Frescatto stormed into the cockpit, followed by Savorelli. "Tell me who would be cooking if I broke my arm instead of my nose? Huh? Monsignors, just look at him. He says he cannot cook because of his broken arm."

"I just asked for help because of my injury," the restaurateur said, confronting his rival. "So what? I tried to secure the hatches."

"It would be better if you secured your ass. We all would be safer," Frescatto snapped and turned to the bishops. "Please excuse me, Monsignors, but it's all because of him, this monster. He fell on me and smashed my face. This bore weighs 200 kilos. He could have crushed me to death."

Francis waved their argument off, pretending to be absorbed by the compass adjustment.

"You both look like you need some rest," Avanella observed.

"How can I take a break from this hippo?" Frescatto asked, pressing a wet rag to his broken nose. "Okay, hippo, let's come downstairs. I'll fix your arm. National *Carabinieri* go through medical training—unlike you, stupid civilian."

"Don't call me a hippo, and don't you dare call me stupid!" Savorelli shouted.

Both men left. The skies cleared after the storm, and Archbishop Avanella gazed at the narrow red stripe bleeding on the horizon, the sunset showing them the way.

The following day, when Bishop Francis's shift at the helm was over and it was time to rest, he remained in the cockpit. Archbishop Avanella took the wheel, seeing that something was bothering his friend.

"Is everything alright, Francis? Nothing wrong with the yacht, I hope?"

"Everything is under control or...almost everything," Francis said, looking sideways at his friend.

"Then, go ahead, shoot. What is bothering you?"

"Well, do you believe in Christ?"

"What?" Avanella was dumbfounded; he expected anything but *this* from his fellow clergyman. "Do I believe in Jesus Christ as our Savior? Yes, absolutely. Otherwise, I wouldn't be here." Avanella eyed Francis. "And so do you, Francis. It's a dumb question unless... Wait a minute, what about you?"

Francis sighed. "I...I don't know anymore. I am trying to keep my faith despite everything that is happening. The Cathedral of John the Baptist in your city is burned to the ground, the *Basilica La Salute* in mine is under water by now, there's no help from Rome, and we're heading across the world on an obscure mission with insufficient force or guidance."

"I thought you were with me," Avanella said after listening carefully. "You were so eager to join us."

"Yes, I was, and I am. It's not that. What we are missing is a *foundation rock*. It's not here anymore." Francis lowered his eyes. "Our generation, all of us, have lost our guidance, our purpose. We left the ground our fathers were standing on and traveled in a shaky boat, both physically and spiritually." He looked at the ever-changing expanse of the ocean around them. "Tell me, what is the Church?"

"The Church is the unifying force. This is the form that unites believers and leads them on an earthly journey. Apostle Peter..."

"Yes, yes," Francis said. "But, the Bible had many authors as we know. The texts we read today were written centuries after Christ, and only a few of these texts were chosen. Who were the judges who selected these books?"

"Well, as you know, all twenty-seven books of the New Testament were written in Greek originally and based on eyewitness accounts. The present New Testament canon was accepted by the Early Church in the fourth century, although all of the dogmatic principles of the canon for our church were not concluded, if I remember correctly, until the Canon of Trent in the sixteenth century."

"Exactly—centuries and centuries after Christ. So, we cannot and should not pretend these books are actual historical documents, because they are not."

"What does it change?" Avanella eyed Francis.

"It means they are only meant for guidance, not axioms. They help us find our way in life as long as we believe these biblical accounts. When everything is stable, it is fine, but what if the earth shakes or the land disappears from under our feet and we find ourselves, as we do now, in the middle of the ocean? Where is our spiritual compass?"

"I see what you mean," Avanella said. "I think, in the end, with all the knowledge we have…" He paused. "We must follow the dictates of our hearts. It is what we believe in, what we think is right…and good for the world."

"Yes, this compass will never betray us." Francis still had a puzzled look. "Avanella, please be frank with me, I must ask you…"

Archbishop Avanella had anticipated the key question his friend still had.

"I heard a rumor that fishermen brought it to Venice. Well, are we going on the mission to save your parishioners and retrieve the Holy Relic, or do we have a bigger plan—to free the Messiah?"

Avanella was at a loss for words. This was the secret that

Giovanni told him—that the image of the Messiah appeared to the watchman before his death.

"Why did you hide it from me?" Francis pressed him.

Avanella was silent.

"Because you never asked," he said finally. "Forgive me."

Francis lowered his head. "We are going to be excommunicated! Do you know that?"

Avanella looked his friend in the eyes.

"Everything will be fine, you will see." He smiled. "Speaking of excommunication, why don't you get some sleep? We'll have a good breakfast then. Our pair of 'frenemies' is cooking something special today."

CHAPTER 40
PREPARING THE IMPOSSIBLE

"WHERE IS HE? WHAT HAPPENED?" Meg kept asking as they returned to the hotel after waiting for Lucas inside the Colosseum.

"I warned him not to venture outside into the crowd," Thomas said, checking his pager. "Oh...here... They just announced that someone was arrested today, a terrorist from Europe."

"It's him!" Meg said. "But he is not a terrorist—they are! Do something. It's your city!"

"What can I do?" Thomas shrugged. "What can anyone do in this situation?"

Meg clenched her fists. "Listen, enough! We sit here and do nothing, and they are about to kill Lucas—and to kill anyone who disagrees with them and their orders." She grabbed Thomas by the collar of his shirt. "Wake up! It's time to act, old man, not to sit on your hands!"

"Thank you for calling me an old man," Thomas uttered, trying to break free from the former swimming champion's grip. "Let me see what I can do...like nothing, really..." He clearly did not want to get even deeper into the risky business, but Meg had nowhere to retreat.

"Do I have to kill you?" she asked. Continuing to hold the concierge, she reached out to the desk and took out Lucas's handgun. "It has only one bullet, but it's enough for you."

"I'm impressed," the concierge said. "It shows your talent as an actress, but killing me won't solve any of our problems."

"I know," Meg said, lowering the gun. "Will you help me or not?"

"That's a more reasonable question," the old professor said with relief. "I definitely will if I only find a way to do it." He went to the window and became lost in thought looking out at the city. "The SS keeps all of those arrested at an airport building, and it's impossible to escape from there unless we have…a plane."

"What? Where would we get a plane?" Meg asked.

"Maybe not a real one," the old concierge remarked. "I know someone who used to run a virtual air show."

"How will a *virtual* plane help him? Can Lucas fly away on it?"

"Probably not, but it will cause a major alarm in the prison, and this will give him a chance to escape." Thomas paused. "Remember, Vega City was built on illusions. Sometimes, this virtual reality is bigger than real life."

"I know," Meg sighed. "My own life was built on it."

"It is sad." Thomas eyed her. "I hope it is starting to change. Well, I'm afraid it's time for me to get back to my duties."

He went to the exit, paused, and looked back at her.

"But first, let me make you something to eat. You're probably hungry."

"Thank you, Thomas," Meg said.

"Don't mention it." The old man chuckled. "And, keep that toy of yours handy." He pointed at Lucas's pistol. "Better safe than sorry." He stopped at the door and asked, "Would you really shoot me if I refused to help him?"

"In a heartbeat," she said, and they both laughed.

"I thought so," he said.

Meg gave him a thankful look. "If your plan works, I'll be calling you Saint Thomas."

He smiled. "And I will call you M. M.—Maria Magdalene."

"Yeah, right." Meg shook her head. "Give me a break. You might as well call me Marilyn Monroe. "

"No, I mean it," Thomas said, leaving the room.

"I don't want it! Who needs to have this name *now*? It's a curse, not a blessing!" Meg said. The door was ajar, but Thomas was gone. She realized that she was talking to herself.

———

The entrance gate to an old farm outside the city still bore a sign: "Pearl Harbor, December 7, 1941—a date that will live in infamy. Admission: $20." A crude image of a Japanese fighter plane, a Mitsubishi Zero, crowned the sign. It had faded over the years, making it appear that the plywood fighter was about to crash-land on the dusty road under the sign. Thomas stopped his bicycle to see the sign better. The ticket price was still in dollars. It was a golden time when the world was still living its normal life, but the presentiment of impending catastrophe was already in the air. It had become popular to recreate manmade disasters using the latest technology: the sinking of the Titanic, the fiery wreck of the Zeppelin Hindenburg, and the September 11 disaster. The Japanese attack on Pearl Harbor was in the same infamous category that brought in good money while the dollar was still high.

Thomas examined the farm. It didn't look like anyone lived there.

"Hey, anyone home?" He walked through the gate to see inside. His plan was falling apart even before it started. An old cast-iron bathtub by the barn was filled with rancid water, showing no sign that anyone used it for the vegetable garden or animals. A ramshackle chicken coop stood empty; only a few feathers stained with chicken manure in the yellow grass showed it was once occupied. The dog-food bowls were empty, and the roof over abandoned horse stables appeared to be on the verge of collapse.

Thomas headed to the main house. The wind blew dry feathery grass around the yard as he approached a dilapidated hut with what used to be a porch in front.

"Knock, knock! Anyone home?" Thomas yelled and suddenly felt that he was being watched. "Alex, are you there? It's Thomas, your former professor," he said, feeling uneasy. *Now, I'm going to be shot for trespassing*, he thought. "Alex, do you hear me?"

He took a few more steps as a huge dark figure blocked his way—a Japanese medieval warrior in full samurai armor who pointed his sword at his face.

"Hi there," Thomas said.

The warrior yelled something in Japanese. It was obviously a command and didn't bode well. *How was this possible in the twenty-first century?* Thomas wondered.

"Don't move... What do you want?" the warrior said in English before he burst out in laughter. "Mr. Thomas, my God! Come on in."

Seems like I am in a James Bond movie, Thomas thought. He was old enough to remember those flicks. He watched as the samurai figure slowly dissolved in the air. Alex stood in the doorway, waving his hand. Short and red-haired with a freckled face, he had not changed much since he was his student at Nevada Tech College.

"I see that you were impressed with my toys," Alex said when Thomas stepped in. "I don't have much functioning equipment left, but it's still enough for a small attraction. What do you have in mind?"

Thomas eyed his former student for several moments. "I will tell you what 'attraction' I have in mind," he said. "But remember, if you agree to help us, our lives will depend on your skills."

CHAPTER 41

NEW AMSTERDAM

AFTER WEEKS of sailing the endless ocean, the crew of *Santa Maria* began to suspect that something was wrong. Only Bishop Francis kept an expression of confidence on his weathered face. For days, he was at the helm and slept on the captain's bridge on a makeshift bed.

Avanella watched his friend with growing doubt. Does he really know where they are sailing? Avanella didn't trust the old compass that Francis was using. Who knows where he got it—maybe at a junkyard. Where were they headed instead of New Amsterdam? The South Pole? Their food reserves were running low and so was the drinking water. Also, almost the entire crew suffered from seasickness, including Savorelli and Frescatto. Both were barely alive.

Avanella climbed the captain's bridge. "Listen, Francis, I was patient and didn't question how you calculated our course using this vintage compass. I presumed it was correct."

The bishop glared at him.

"But now, after weeks of traveling, I need to see the chart and your calculations," Avanella said, feeling increasingly uncomfortable under his friend's stare. "I found a course calculation manual in the yacht's documents. Show me the course. I need to check it."

Bishop Francis turned away, looking into the endless distance of the ocean. *"As they sailed he fell asleep and there came down a storm of wind…and they were in jeopardy. And they came to him, and awoke him, saying, Master, master, we perish. Then he arose, and rebuked the wind and the raging of the water and they ceased, and there was a calm. And he said unto them, you whose faith is weak, where is your faith?"*

"Luke 8:25," Avanella said. "It's so true, and we should always remember this, but now I…"

"Don't say anything if you still want us to be friends," Francis said. "I cherish your friendship, and it would be very painful to lose it."

"More than friendship…brotherhood," Avanella said.

"Indeed." Francis looked into his eyes. "Do you think I would put in jeopardy all these people who trusted me with their lives? Including you?"

"No, but…."

"Then go back to the crew, calm them down, and let me do my job," he said."Please!"

It was early morning two days later when the tired crew was asleep as someone touched Avanella on the shoulder.

"What? What happened?" Avanella opened his eyes. Francis stared at him.

"What, Francis?"

Francis remained silent.

"What happened? Emergency? We ran aground?"

"New Amsterdam is on the horizon." A happy smile lit up his friend's face. "We made it!"

CHAPTER 42

GREAT ESCAPE

BY THE END of the week, the death cell where they kept infected prisoners fell silent. No moans or pleas for mercy were coming out of it. Now the time had come to harvest the dead bodies. For this purpose, the SS guards used luggage carts, which were in abundance at the airport.

Goliath, wearing a protective suit, headed to the cell door with a dozen guards.

"Get ready, put your masks on," he said in a rumbling voice. The Centurion was about to give the command to open the cell as the soldier at the door took off his mask.

"I...I can't breathe..." he mumbled, collapsing on the floor.

"Jason lost his mask yesterday," the other guard said. "He said it was optional anyway."

"Check if he's still alive," Goliath ordered.

The guard touched the sick man with his glove.

"Well?"

"I don't think he's alive. I don't feel his pulse, sir," the guard said. "But my gloves are too thick."

"Never mind." Goliath turned to his frightened men.

"You see what happens when you don't follow orders?

The virus will kill you before I do. Who wants to be next? Anyone?"

"Throw him in with the rest of the dead," Goliath said, removing the AK-47 machine gun from his shoulder. A bayonet was attached to its muzzle; the Centurion ran his weapon through the soldier's body." Yes, he is dead alright." He turned to the rest of the team. "Go on, move!"

Entering the cell, the guards started throwing the bodies on luggage carts that they brought with them. Goliath waited by the door, piercing each body with a bayonet before he allowed the dead prisoner to be taken away.

"Are the undertakers ready downstairs?" Goliath asked, escorting the first cart on the way to the body disposal area, which used to be the airport luggage hall.

"Yes, Centurion," the chief undertaker said, switching on a conveyor belt. The limp bodies flopped on it and disappeared in the mechanical bowels of the sorting machine.

"Do you think it's just a virus? Or is it something else, like the bubonic plague? I see more and more bodies charred by it like fire," the officer said, checking his gas mask.

"I don't give a rat's crap!" Goliath said, returning to his team.

Their work continued until the cell was cleared of decaying bodies. Inspecting the last cart, Goliath was going to give the command to roll it away when something stopped him. He couldn't say what it was, but something was not right with this load. He checked the bodies, peering into the dead faces. Some were calm as if accepting their fate, some were tense as if they were still going through their torment, some exhibited open eyes— struggling to ask the last question that they had never had a chance to ask before. But, there was one more face. The Centurion bent over it so close that he almost touched it as he peered at its features—but then he saw a drop of sweat trickle down the dead man's temple.

"So, you're still alive!" Goliath said.

The would-be escapee opened his eyes. Blood flowed from the wound on his shoulder made by Goliath's blade.

"Well, say something before I kill you," the Centurion said. "How did you stay alive? Everyone is dead in this room."

"I'm the only survivor," said the prisoner in a weak voice.

"Not for long…" Goliath put his bayonet to his throat. "What's your name?"

"Dr. Portnoy from Nazareth."

"Why didn't you die with everyone? Speak before I cut your head off!"

"Because…I…have tasted His wine, the blood of my Lord."

"You're lying. I think I'll still cut off your head." Goliath pressed the bayonet to Portnoy's throat, drawing blood. "I'll cut you into pieces and make you eat each of them until you confess."

"Then kill me, the one who has a cure for the virus…" The prisoner closed his eyes.

The Centurion studied him. Although the prisoner had tried to hold on bravely, drops of sweat trickled down his face, an unmistakable sign of fear.

Goliath turned to his team.

"Handcuff him and bring him to headquarters. No excessive torture; I need him to speak."

Goliath went to the disposal department.

"Instruct the guards outside to shoot each corpse through the head before they get rid of them," he told the chief undertaker. "I don't trust these walking dead."

———

Lucas opened his eyes and found himself on a conveyor belt among other bodies. The belt wasn't moving. He lay motionless, trying not to attract the attention of the guards. Why this pause? He felt a sharp pain in his upper chest, possibly from the stabbing wound, but he couldn't move to see what it was. Finally, the blood-soaked belt came to life, pulling him through the tunnel and out of the building. The daylight at the end of the tunnel came closer as he heard the sound of gunshots coming from the airfield. Lucas realized that this was the final "control check"—death guaranteed. Overcoming his pain, Lucas climbed over the bodies behind him, trying to get back inside the terminal, but the conveyor belt kept moving. For several minutes, he stayed in one place, struggling desperately and feeling the last of his strength dissipate. He finally collapsed on the moving belt and closed his eyes. The shots were getting closer. The conveyor belt was about to spit him out onto the receiving platform to certain death.

Goliath left the airport building and walked to his vehicle. It was a military version of the electric Hummer 0, one of the few produced before the Great Crash. The "0" in its name meant zero emissions, and the high-tech rooftop solar panel provided enough power for a short trip. The Centurion got inside and ordered the driver to go to headquarters as the howl of a diving bomber deafened him. Flashes of fire and smoke clouded the sky. Goliath watched in disbelief over how a Japanese World War II plane could be attacking the airport. One of the bombs exploded in front of the Hummer. The flash blinded him, and the Hummer caught fire. Jumping out of it, the Centurion stood shell-shocked in the midst of the destruction, watching as the guards and technicians fled the airport buildings trying to survive the air raid. Thinking that he was going insane, Goliath covered his face with his huge hands, cursing the cowardly guards and the plane. A minute later, when he took his hands from his face, there were no signs of the attack. No bomb craters were visible on the airfield, and the Hummer was intact.

In an abandoned airport hangar at the other end of the runway, Alex was folding his equipment. He was proud that his air show had worked so well, but now it was time to get out of this place before they were shot by SS guards who would be furious about being fooled. Getting worried, Alex waited for the return of his friends. Had their plan succeeded in freeing the arrested? Where are they? Why are they dragging their feet? Alex was happy to see Thomas and the girl carrying the fugitive on their shoulders. His head fell on his wounded chest, he was bleeding, and his rescuers prayed they could bring him home alive.

CHAPTER 43

GOLIATH'S PLAN

GOLIATH GRADUALLY CAME to his senses. What was it he had just witnessed? He had no answer. The attack was too real to be a mass hallucination, but worst of all, his soldiers proved to be cowards. His driver disappeared, as did the guards at the entrance. The Centurion grabbed one of the deserters who was returning to his post and looked into his eyes. There was fear, blind fear. More than anything, the Centurion hated cowards, who drove him into an uncontrollable rage. He punched the scum in his face, and the guard fell dead against the Hummer, leaving a trail of blood on the passenger door. Something was very wrong, and he must warn the Prefect.

The Colosseum rose before him in a mute greeting as Goliath drove up to the main gate. After weeks of the trial, when crowds had besieged it, the vast premises of the palace were deserted. Ignoring the presence of two guards saluting him, he entered the building. In the eerie silence within, his steps echoed under the arches as he made his way to the stairs—working elevators throughout the city were a thing of the past. After passing several flights of stairs, the Centurion reached the Prefect's private quarters. To his surprise, there were no guards in front of it.

"I salute you, Hegemon!" the Centurion said, stepping inside. The front hall, decorated with ancient Greek statues and mosaics, was empty.

Strange... There is no security at the heart of power, Goliath puzzled, checking other rooms.

"My Leader!" Goliath knocked on the last door.

"Come in, Goliath, and please don't call me that. For you, I'm just Marcus," the voice came from behind the door.

Since when did he become so... welcoming? wondered Goliath. Somewhat confused, the Centurion stepped in. A few candles cast reflections on the red marble walls; a glass door to the garden terrace was wide open. A gust of wind burst into the room.

"Close the door, Goliath. I hate drafts, just like this mysterious virus—it's killing everyone." The Prefect emerged from the garden. He was dressed in a Roman toga and wore soft sandals.

Goliath did not appreciate these attempts to imitate ancient Rome but did not dare to object.

"I'm here to report an incident in the concentration camp. It defies explanation."

The Prefect scanned the room around them, but his eyes, swollen after sleepless nights, showed no interest in the Centurion's report.

"Or is it that *you* just can't explain it?" he said listlessly, still thinking about something of his own.

"This was an air attack! The entire airport was on fire and..."

"Shush," said Marcus, waving his hand to silence him. "Aren't you surprised by not seeing anyone here? Why am I alone?"

"Well..." Goliath began. "Yes, I thought..."

"I'll tell you why." The Prefect took a few steps towards

him and then abruptly recoiled as if faced with fire or a poisonous snake. "Because they are dead! Gas masks no longer help. We must stay socially distanced. This is the only solution, doctors say."

"Doctors?" the Centurion said. "What doctors?"

"Doesn't matter…doctors in California. There is no cure for the pandemic. It spreads among the troops like wildfire. No one is safe now."

"But we still need to maintain order, take measures…"

"Yes." Marcus eyed Goliath. "And here's the first step: I decided to end the trial and acquit the defendant. People must stay home to avoid spreading the deadly disease."

"It's impossible," Goliath said. "With all due respect, your soldiers, guards, unions, the whole city expects a death sentence. Anything else will be seen as a sign of weakness!"

"I see this, but I am also responsible for the safety of the people, even if they do not realize it themselves. We are 'Security Servants' after all, don't forget this."

"As you wish," Goliath said slowly, overcoming himself, his protest. "How soon must I announce the verdict?"

"As early as possible. Tomorrow, you will have the text. The plague of the century must be stopped at all costs."

"Does it mean we must shut down the city? It will cause hunger and riots, causing many more people to die or be killed."

"No doubt, but it is a small price to pay. As I said, the verdict will be signed tomorrow, and then it's up to you how well you fulfill my orders." The Perfect looked into the Centurion's eyes. "Do I make myself clear?"

"Yes, Hegemon…Marcus…" Goliath bowed to the supreme leader and was about to leave when a sudden thought stopped him.

"Hegemon… With your permission, I may have the solution. The capital offender will be punished and our troops saved, together with the inhabitants of this doomed city."

CHAPTER 44
LUCAS AND MAGDALENE

LUCAS SLEPT for two days. his face showed signs of torture, he was motionless, and only his eyelids trembled slightly when Meg changed his bandages, indicating that he felt her presence. Thomas assisted Meg. Both were happy to see how quickly Lucas's chest wound was healing.

"Soon, you won't see a thing," Thomas said.

Meg bent over Lucas, looking lovingly into his face. His eyes slowly opened.

"It's you," Lucas said softly. "Am…I dreaming? Or, am I in heaven?"

"It's not a dream," she said. "I am here with you."

"What happened?" Lucas looked around the room. "I remember explosions, fire, and smoke. Was it real too?"

"Not quite, rather a very realistic illusion." Thomas chuckled. "A friend of mine has created this virtual reality. He was the best special effects expert in Hollywood."

Lucas smiled. "I'm afraid to close my eyes," he said. "If I do, this room; you, my love, and you, Thomas will disappear…forever."

Meg took his hand. "I am real, and I will be with you…always."

"Magdalene," he whispered in relief, falling asleep.

CHAPTER 45

SPIRITUAL INVASION

THEY DOCKED IN WEST MANHATTAN. Disabled cruise liners with rusty balconies and broken windows crowded the port area, a reminder of the COVID-19 epidemic that hit the city years before. The Great Digital Crash dealt the final blow.

"I feel like I'm in a graveyard," Francis said, stepping onto a deserted pier. He held one of the fliers that the wind blew across the sidewalk. It read:

*GREAT MEN AND WOMEN OF NEW AMSTERDAM,
OUR HOMES AND LIVES ARE IN JEOPARDY!
ARMIES OF ROGUE BISHOPS ARE CLOSING IN. LED
BY FANATICISM STEMMED IN THE DARK AGES,
THESE MODERN CRUSADERS HAVE NO MERCY
ON THE YOUNG AND SICK, NOR DO THEY
RESPECT OUR DEMOCRATIC VALUES. THE MAYOR
OFFICE ISSUES A CALL TO ARMS!*

*ALL CAPABLE CITIZENS MUST GATHER AT THE
PORT TO DEFEND OUR CITY. ARM YOURSELF AND
FULFILL YOUR CIVIC DUTY!*

"Well, they got everything just about right." Bishop Francis chuckled, passing the flier to his friend. "Indeed, we are those bishops. Finally, I feel important."

Archbishop Avanella just smiled. He had expected a much worse reception and was relieved that his fears had not materialized. Dizzy and walking unsteadily after the long journey, the crew of the *Santa Maria* took to the city streets.

"It's so dark here, it's like a jungle," Savorelli said, staring cautiously at the huge skyscrapers above them. "The sunlight probably never reaches these streets."

"You've made a very important discovery, Savorelli." Frescatto gave him a sarcastic look. "You can also use the phrase, 'concrete jungle.'"

"What? I don't get it." The restaurateur was lost. "What do you mean?"

"Never mind, just keep walking."

The couple led the procession while Avanella and Francis fell behind, checking a paper map of the city they found tacked to an abandoned kiosk. In the dead silence, the sound of their footsteps flew forward, bouncing off the walls.

"I still wonder, where is everybody?" Savorelli cringed. "It's weird."

"Did you see the leaflets? The city folks are probably still searching for weapons to fight us."

"What do you mean? Weren't they all disarmed years ago to reduce city crime?" Savorelli said. "I read it in *La Stampa* when my favorite paper was still circulating."

"That's exactly what I mean." His partner eyed him and waved his hand hopelessly. "You don't get it anyway."

They both slowed their steps when they saw a lone figure at the end of the street, a man in his thirties wearing a paramilitary jacket and khaki pants. He stood silently, waiting for them to come closer.

"I bet this is a white supremacist," Savorelli whispered. "I've read about them."

"I don't see any weapon on him," Frescatto said. "Maybe he has a pocket knife or something, but that's all."

Savorelli cheered up on hearing this but, just in case, glanced back to make sure the others were following. He approached the stranger.

"How do you do?" the restaurateur said in English, which he'd learned ages ago in school.

"Hi," the man said. "Are you rogue bishops?"

"Well…" Frescatto began.

"Yes, today is a beautiful day," Savorelli interrupted him proudly.

"Are you sure you're *those* bishops?" The man glanced at the rest of their team. "Those two people behind you look more like clergy, but there's still no way you could all pass for crusaders."

"Are you disappointed?" Avanella asked, catching up with them.

"Maybe not, I'm not quite sure." The stranger smiled. "We expected an army with weapons, crosses…all the invasion paraphernalia."

"Then consider it a rather small spiritual conquest," Avanella said. "I am Archbishop Avanella."

"Victor. Pleasure to meet you all."

After weeks of danger and suffering, they found themselves in a lavish cupola mansion atop one of New Amsterdam's most iconic buildings. The only working elevator in the city transported them there. The *Santa Maria* crew was stunned to see the interior.

"It's…so opulent," Bishop Francis said when he took in the vast open space filled with antique furniture, old books, and musical instruments. "It reminds me of a medieval palazzo in my native Venice before the flood. Did you *buy* all this?"

"I found it," the host said. "This is one of the few perks of living in a dead city, even though you risk your life along the way."

"Why are you calling this city dead?" Avanella asked. "Where is everybody?"

"Most of them are in their graves—those lucky ones who have them. Others died on the street or fled, fearing the invasion."

"*Our* invasion?" Francis asked.

"*Si,*" Victor nodded.

"You know Italian?"

"Not really, but my friend taught me some," Victor said.

"Who is your friend?"

"I'm not at liberty to say." Victor hesitated.

"Why?"

"Because he asked me."

"Is his name Lucas?" Archbishop Avanella eyed the host.

"I...I don't know."

"As you wish. Keep it secret," Avanella said and paused. "We came to save him, and your information would be very valuable."

"Well, he is not here, that's all I can say." Victor looked doubtful at the deranged travelers who looked more like a bunch of mental patients than warriors. "Your first priority should be to avoid getting infected with the virus, which destroyed this city. It will kill you before you can help anyone."

"We are ready to take our chances," Avanella said. "With your help or without it. Maybe you can still tell us where Lucas is?"

"Well, he's in Vega City," Victor said after a long pause. "He must be sick. Everyone is dying there."

"Please, tell us everything you know," Avanella asked.

"The information I have is sketchy. First, you need to realize that you're facing two enemies: the Killer Virus and Security Servants. Both are deadly. You will need antivirus gear and weapons to fight the SS. I don't believe you have any."

"Can we get something at city hospitals?" Francis said.

Victor turned to him. "No, all the hospitals are ransacked. You won't find anything there except some uncollected corpses."

"How about weapons at a SWAT arsenal?" Francis asked.

Victor shook his head. "Everything is gone. The living have looted everything. I may be able to manufacture a couple of handguns on my 3D printer, but it won't help much."

The bishops exchanged looks. This was the defining moment of their expedition.

"Is there any vaccine or cure for this virus?" Avanella asked.

Victor shook his head. "The longer you stay in this city, the higher the chance of contracting the virus. You'll be dead in two days. And, if you go to Vega City, the SS will kill you there at once."

"I don't like it," Francis sighed. "There must be some way out. I cannot imagine dying in this horrible place."

"We have two choices," Avanella said. "Collect as much food as possible and return home on our wrecked yacht, or continue the journey no matter what, hoping for God's help."

"I prefer the second option, as shaky as it may be, but we've got to put it to a vote before the crew," Francis said. "These are their lives at stake, and they must decide for themselves."

"I agree," Avanella said. "If they choose to return, God save their souls without a skipper..." He paused and looked at Francis. "Then you will go with them, Francis, and I'll continue the expedition alone."

"Totally unacceptable." Francis shook his head stubbornly. "Together we stand, together we fall."

"Let's not argue," said Avanella. "Let's hear what the crew has to say."

Avanella trusted his men, and their vote was predictable. Nearly all of them favored continuing their quest. Only Mario, the youngest man in the team, disagreed. Being recently married with his wife expecting a child, he had soon regretted his decision to join the mission. He realized that his family was more important. The farther from home, the more acutely he felt it.

Once again, Avanella was in a difficult situation. Sending the young man back alone was impossible.

"I see only one solution," Avanella said. "If our host doesn't object, Mario can stay here until our return. In the meantime, another ship might arrive and take him home." The archbishop looked at Victor. "What do you say, our generous friend? At last, you'll have company."

"I don't mind," Victor said. "Someone will look after my place while I'm gone. I'll go with you, bishops…um, what does the crew call you, monsignors? Will you take me?"

Avanella and Francis exchanged dubious looks, and it took them a while to respond. Finally, Avanella walked over to Victor and shook his hand. "I didn't realize how many crazy people are still in this world." He chuckled. "Now, we only need to find a way to get to Vega City."

CHAPTER 46
BLOOD MONEY

CENTURION GOLIATH LEFT the palace in high spirits. He finally knew what needed to be done. The tired and demoralized Prefect gave him freedom of action, and Goliath was not going to miss his chance. Driving to headquarters, he saw bodies lying on the street, no one daring to collect them. The epidemic had struck Vega City with devastating force, and whoever stops it will be awarded full power over the city and the entire state.

Arriving at the black pyramid of the Pharaoh Casino, which served as headquarters, the Centurion flew into a rage upon not seeing any sentries along the perimeter of the building.

"Guards!" shouted Goliath, bursting inside.

A frightened legionnaire appeared before him. He was in a state of panic, and his hands were shaking.

"Where are the others?" the Centurion said, hearing the echo of his voice.

"Dead," the officer said. "The virus killed them."

"Did they wear gloves and masks?"

"Masks don't help, sir. The virus passes through any protection," the officer said, breathing heavily. "We will all die soon."

"Sooner than you think!" The Centurion grabbed the coward by the throat. He was about to smash his head against the wall, but stopped, realizing that he would soon find himself without his soldiers. "Bring me the arrested doctor," the Centurion said. "And, gather all who are still alive."

When the guards brought the prisoner to the command post, the Centurion looked into his face again. Exhausted by torture and hunger, the doctor bore no trace of the deadly disease.

"Follow me," Goliath told the arrested. "You stay here," he ordered the soldiers.

Stopping and stumbling from weakness, Portnoy followed the giant. They went through the upper gallery to the Maya pyramid, which featured a stairway in front that extended to the very top of the structure.

"What do you see?" Goliath said when they reached the peak.

"I can hardly see anything. My cell was dark, and my eyes ache from the light," Portnoy said. "It's very high up here. That's all I can say."

"This pyramid was brought here from Mexico. Ancient Mayans sacrificed enemy warriors on it, tearing out their hearts. And your friend, whom you call the Lord and others call the Messiah, was going down these stairs to the believers. You drank His wine, and it saved you. Now, it's time to tell me what this wine is made of."

Portnoy hesitated.

"I'll make it easier for you." Goliath grabbed the arrested and lifted him over the edge. "It's a long way down. I hope you can see it now."

"Please…" Portnoy pleaded. "I will tell you everything I know."

"That's better. Don't make me regret that I spared your life."

Portnoy fell to his knees when the Centurion pulled him back.

"Tell me what I already know. I need to hear it from you," Goliath said.

"He used his blood and water to make this wine." Portnoy spoke hastily, fearing he would be interrupted. "I don't know the exact proportion, but I think that just a few drops were enough to produce a large amount of wine. Its effect is immediate, but one must not drink too much because you can get an overdose, and then the consequences are unpredictable."

"You will be in charge, and you will get enough blood. I will see to it."

"*His* blood?"

"*His.*"

"I...I can't." The doctor's eyes filled with fear.

"You can't, or you won't?"

The doctor was sweating.

"Well, we've already wasted too much time." Goliath put his hand on the doctor's head. "I'll crash your little brain in one move."

"No, no, you misunderstood me. I don't refuse, I just don't know where to start," Portnoy said.

"You will start in His cell. Then I'll find another place." The Centurion loomed over him. "Take as much blood as you need. The High Prefect sentenced Him to death anyway."

The next day, the long-awaited verdict was announced. It read:

THE PREFECT OF NEVADA AND CALIFORNIA
EXAMINED THE CASE OF THE DEFENDANT,
KNOWN AS J. C., AND FOUND NO *CORPUS
DELICTI* IN HIS ACTIONS.

HOWEVER, TAKING INTO ACCOUNT THAT THE
MIRACULOUS CURE CAN ONLY BE ATTRIBUTED
TO A HIGHER POWER, COMMONLY KNOWN AS
GOD, THE PREFECT FINDS THE ACCUSED GUILTY
OF SO-CALLED "ACTS OF GOD," INCLUDING THE
CURRENT PANDEMIC, WHICH IS DESTROYING
THE CITY POPULATION AND COSTING THOU-
SANDS OF LIVES.

THE PREFECT CONDEMNS THE ACCUSED TO
EXSANGUINATION TO PREVENT FURTHER
SPREAD OF THE DISEASE AND COMPENSATE THE
POPULATION FOR THE DAMAGE CAUSED BY IT.

THIS VERDICT IS FINAL AND NOT SUBJECT TO
APPEAL.

Pete Gronovski, the Workers Coalition chief, and John (aka Johnny the Baptist), head of the newly-created Union of Reformed Religious Activists, received the verdict with relief. The trial that had rocked Vega City for weeks was finally over. It was time to get back to normal, which in their case always meant making more money.

"It was an excellent idea to get us all unionized," John said, sitting in Gronovski's new office. "Together, we have a much stronger voice in the city's affairs."

"You got lucky you avoided prosecution," Gronovski reminded him. "Religion is out of fashion now and may soon be totally banned."

"Maybe so, but didn't it make us both a lot of money?" The post-religious activist, as John now called himself, put an envelope with e-coins on the chairman's desk. "This is your share of the court's admission fee."

"How much is here?"

"It doesn't matter, it's all yours." John eyed Gronovski. "You won't be disappointed."

"Yeah, I know, but what if the SS finds out? They control the city."

"They are busy with other affairs. There is a power struggle between the First Centurion and the High Prefect. The one is young and full of energy; the other is old and may soon leave. Our hands are free to start a new business."

"What's that?" Pete asked incredulously. It was difficult for him to keep up with the quick-thinking partner.

"Set a price for healing. His blood works wonders. All civilians will have to pay, say, two hundred per person."

"Just add another one hundred to my share," Gronovski said. "Human life is worth it."

———

On a day marked by the solstice and spring thunderstorms, guards entered the high-security block in the Human Shelter and dragged the convicted onto a bus waiting outside. Its destination was a former airbase near the city, commonly known as Area 51. This location had long passed its heyday as a cradle for extraterrestrial conspiracy theories, and its funding went dry with the decline of federal power in Washington. Left to negligence and disrepair, the Area 51 installations crumpled under the merciless Nevada sun, and it's only surviving structure was the Tower, a huge monolith rumored to be guarding the entrance to the secret facilities.

In the upper part of the tower was a large circular hall with a sculpture in the form of a cross made of shiny metal beams in the middle. It symbolized the human quest for contact with other worlds, but was unfinished, missing the central human figure, and was abandoned like the rest of the base. The convicted was fastened to the cross for the procedure of exsanguination. Dozens of rubber tubes extended to his arms and legs. He was blindfolded. Dr. Portnoy insisted on this because neither he nor his assistants could bear the mournful gaze of the condemned man.

I only fulfill my duties as a doctor, Portnoy told himself, driving away the thought that he had become an executioner. *If not me, then others will make it more painful. This is necessary to save human lives, thousands of lives that would otherwise be lost.* Yet, despite all his efforts, the doctor was experiencing an excruciating sense of guilt and, more than once, caught himself thinking that it would probably be better to die that day in the prison cell along with all the others affected by the terrible disease.

The blood of the convicted was drained into metal containers and distributed to the population in small portions mixed with water. The guards were the first to receive the vaccine; they combed the city, looking for the sick. Every resident was required to be vaccinated and could not refuse to pay. Money flowed into the city treasury.

CHAPTER 47

WHERE ARE ALL THE HEALED?

"JUST AS I PREDICTED, they sentenced Him to death. I was right, unfortunately," Thomas said as he and Meg were caring for Lucas, who had developed a fever. The escapee lay on the hotel bed with his eyes closed and seemed to be asleep. His breathing was rapid as if he was reliving what had happened to him. At this moment, Meg could not think of anyone but her loved one.

"He cannot die... The blood of the Lord is in him," she said, trying to spot signs of improvement in Lucas's face.

Realizing that they were talking about different things, the professor fell silent. He was not sure that the young woman fully understood what had happened to J. C.—that a death sentence had been ordered, even though it was disguised by those who reasoned it would benefit the city's suffering population.

"It's not safe here," Thomas said. "We must leave. It's better to get him out of town."

"Why? This hotel is officially closed," she noted.

"Maybe, but the SS may check it anyway." Thomas came to the window and looked outside. "They destroy entire neighborhoods infected with the virus if there are too many deceased. Alex's farm is the safer place."

"But how do we manage to take Lucas out?" Meg turned to him as if trying to read the answer on his gaunt face.

"I'll think of something," the professor said. "This city has many underground tunnels. I'll have to find the right one."

"And I must find that girl..." Meg looked at the old man. "Remember, that strange man told Lucas that she has a mission to save the Messiah."

"Yes, I remember, but who knows—maybe it just seemed to our friend that he was talking to someone. He barely survived his ordeal," Thomas said. "Also, we have not found thousands of believers healed by J. C."

"Why do you still call Him by those initials?" Meg looked at him.

"Because I don't believe in miracles," the professor admitted. "It contradicts everything I've seen in my long life."

"You never change, do you?" Meg said. "Don't you really care what happened before your eyes—the appearance of the Messiah—and the hatred of the people around him? Their cruelty?"

"Oh yes, I do believe in human cruelty. It is limitless and all-consuming. The Bible is full of these examples, as is the history of mankind," Thomas said. "I believe in this because it reflects the true face of man—who he is and not as we want to see him: sweet and kind beyond belief, soaring in the clouds."

"It's very difficult to live thinking this way," Meg said, "if all you see are the bestial faces. As for myself, I feel that I have completely changed. It seems to me that I have become better in overcoming my doubts and temptations."

"There are no temptations left in this cursed city," said Thomas with bitterness in his voice.

"Despair is one of them," she reminded him.

"Well, maybe you are right... Getting desperate doesn't really help." He paused. "So, where are you planning to look for that girl?"

"I don't know, not just yet. But I hope that my feminine intuition will help me find her."

"It doesn't sound too encouraging if you are only hoping to rely on your intuition. You don't know the city." Thomas eyed her. "Stay here while I'll check something. I may know the place."

He put on his jacket, took the cane he had been using lately, opened the door—and grabbed his chest.

"It's something wrong... My heart—it just stopped for a moment," he said, falling on a chair and catching his breath. "I haven't been to a doctor for quite some time, but where would I find one?" He paused, listening to the pain in his chest.

"I'm afraid you will have to go instead of me." The professor looked at Meg. "I am sorry, my daughter. Old age is not a joy, at least in my case."

CHAPTER 48
THE DYING CITY

THE VIEW of the city from Caesar Palace was ominous. black smoke rose over entire districts struck by the pandemic. Although dozens of sanitary squads delivered the vaccine, the disease did not recede, more and more areas were contaminated, and guards armed with flamethrowers burned the dead. No one knew if there was enough blood for the vaccine to turn the tide.

The Prefect observed the efforts to fight the disease from the roof terrace of his palace and had little hope for success. He made the decision to return to California. His task was completed—crime was punished and control over the population was restored— even though the city would be dead at the end of the day. In his heart, he detested this city with all of its intrigues, corrupt authorities, and anonymous complaints about him, which flowed from here to the Supreme Consul. The real power was in California, not in this leprosy-like nightmare.

"Summon the First Centurion," the Prefect ordered the chief of security. He looked into the face of the old warrior. Jorgen had been through every conflict on the planet, from the wars in Iraq and Afghanistan to the bombings of Syria and Iran. He escaped all of them unharmed but had nearly died recently of the Killer Virus. The miracle vaccine saved him.

"Your method apparently works," the Prefect said when Goliath entered the office.

"It's just my duty, nothing else." Goliath saluted the Prefect.

"What is the situation in the city? Some say we may still lose the battle."

"The situation improves, but slowly. If only we had enough blood at the source. My people drain it in small portions; we try to save as much of it as possible."

"Good, then I appoint you military ruler of the city in my absence."

"Is the Hegemon leaving town?"

"Yes, I see no more need for my presence here. I depart today."

"Why such a rush, may I ask?"

"State affairs in California. By the way, did you find out who was behind the attack on the airport?"

"Not yet, but I have a team of investigators working on it."

"Is anyone missing among the prisoners? Dead or alive?"

"One is not accounted for." The Centurion hesitated. "Or rather, his corpse."

"How did it happen?"

"In the course of the attack. We're working to establish details."

"Could this be a prison break?"

"I don't think so. It cannot be done."

"And yet, check this possibility."

"I understand, Hegemon. Will there be anything else?"

"That's all. You can go now."

Leaving the palace, Goliath remembered the doctor, a failed fugitive who knew much more than anyone could have guessed. Well, this secret will cost him dearly, he thought. It was time to find out what else the doctor might have in mind.

"To Area 51, quick!" he ordered the driver.

They sped through the deserted streets, lit by fire. Sanitary teams in black overalls and gas masks were pulling burnt corpses from under the rubble. The city convulsed, trying to overcome the terrible disease. The final outcome was unclear.

CHAPTER 49
JOURNEY TO THE
CENTER OF THE EARTH

ALTHOUGH THE FIRST Gravity-Vacuum Transit or GVT concept dated back to the early 60s, its first large-scale implementation did not take place until 2010. It received a Top Secret code and was created for the purpose of discreet rapid deployment of troops from coast to coast. The funding was massive, but both the project and its final result remained virtually unknown until the collapse of the Federal Government and its institutions. Subsequently, the project's technical data started popping up in scattered pieces in open sources. The characteristics were futuristic. Each capsule containing 100 soldiers was capable of reaching a top speed of 1,000 miles per hour. This was a mind-blowing achievement for ground or rather underground transportation because it was carried out in a network of underground tubes. The fantastic nature of the project and its existence sounded so out of this world that almost no one among the general population believed it.

Twenty-plus years after the completion of the project, hardly anyone knew where the mysterious route started in the East and where it ended in the West, and it took Victor several days to solve this riddle.

Why am I helping these crazy padres? They will be killed, and so will I. Victor wandered, but could not help himself, carried away by their insane belief in the possibility of their enterprise.

Finally, on a cold early morning, Victor announced to his guests that he had found the way to ferry them west. It didn't take them long to get ready and, laden with food and clothing, they trudged through the streets to Manhattan Bridge, a rusty multilevel structure over the East River. Everyone felt like a bunch of Boy Scouts, albeit headed to imminent death.

This is some kind of child sacrifice, Francis thought.

To distract himself from these thoughts, he asked Victor about the transport they were about to use.

"So, this is a cylinder, you say?"

"A cylinder."

"And it will carry us all the way across the country?"

"It should... I hope."

"It must be some kind of miracle unless, of course, it's a hoax. How did you find it?"

"That's a good question, padre—sorry, Your Eminence." Victor was happy to keep the conversation going. "This was the main problem. Where was it to be found? Certainly at one of the abandoned subway stations because it was a secret project. Right?"

"Probably. How do I know?"

"Here, the most obvious choice would be the Old City Hall station, an iconic architectural gem shown occasionally to tourists. But I knew it would be too easy, too obvious, so which one? There are dozens of abandoned stations under the city."

"*All* of the stations are not in use now. There is no power. You told me this, Victor."

"Yes, it makes it even more difficult."

They reached Worth Street and turned left into Lower Manhattan.

"And then I remembered the Beach Pneumatic Transit

project," Victor continued. "Believe it or not, it ran success-fully for three years, starting in 1870, alas only along one city block. The new tunnel must be somewhere near, I thought, and sure enough, I found it! Ironically, this was right under the Municipal Archives vault where I unearthed its technical details."

They came to a vast brick building, its windows boarded up with plywood.

"Here it is," Victor said. He led them to the service entrance and lifted the metal door in the floor with a crowbar. "It took me a while to break the lock. It's called criminal tres-passing. Step in…" He disappeared into a dark hole, and they followed the beam of his flashlight. Inside, they saw steps leading into the depths of the building's basement. They went down and stopped in front of a wall of cement blocks.

"That's it, here!" Victor said solemnly, pointing to the dead end.

"Here…what?" Francis was surprised. "This passage is walled up. I doubt we have heavy equipment to break through this wall."

"We won't need it." Their guide enjoyed their confusion. "*Vu a la!*" He pushed the wall with his hand, and the gray blocks fell to the floor on the other side. "It is plastic, created only to give the impression of a wall that can be removed in a minute to use the transit capsule."

"You're just an overgrown kid," Francis grumbled as they climbed over the blocks.

"I still don't understand how we may use this derelict device," Avanella said when they approached a thirty-foot-long steel capsule positioned in front of a round tunnel.

"Where would we get the electrical current to power it?"

"Good question," Victor said, opening the sliding door panel. "This tunnel, we call it a tube, is dug in a straight line from the East Coast to the West, and due to the bending of the earth's surface, gravity itself accelerates and then slows down the capsule. So, not much power is needed—only enough to create sufficient magnetic levitation, which we call Maglev, to keep the capsule afloat."

Now we are going to hear a full lecture on physics and the technical wonders of this decaying city, Francis thought in painful anticipation.

Victor caught his eye. "But, I don't want to bore your grace with it. Long story short, the rarefied atmosphere is already created in the GVT tube, which reduces air resistance, allowing the capsule to travel at such high speeds."

"But what about…" the bishop started.

"Power? You're absolutely right. We still need electricity or rather a pocket of power to feed the GVT system, and it is provided by a special military-grade generator, completely isolated from the city power grid or any outside de-energized utility systems. It works on the principle of temperature difference, but more on that some other time. The important thing is that the system has active and ultra-high-capacity batteries on the moving module fully charged.That's all the power we need… I think."

"So, you are not sure?" Avanella joined them.

"Yes, I am… eighty percent," said the young man.

Bishops silently shivered, as if a cold wind had blown on them.

As they were taking their seats, Savorelli bent down to the inspector and handed him a yellowed piece of paper. "Look what I found in his apartment," Savorelli whispered.

It was an article from an old issue of the *New Amsterdam Times:*

Police found the body in Lower Manhattan. According to police sources, the CEO of the electronic company Big Apple, Victor Adams, 29, was the victim of a burglary gone wrong. The victim returned home as criminals were breaking into his four-story apartment, seizing electronics and other valuable items. Anyone with information about this case is strongly advised to contact the police homicide hotline.

"Should I give it to the archbishop?" Savorelli asked.

"Nah, it's some kind of a mistake. We shouldn't bother the monsignor with this." Frescatto crumpled the paper in his fist and shoved it under his seat. Both looked at Victor, who activated the control panel, which illuminated their faces with a ghostly light. "Aha, it works."

"It looks like a sci-fi movie," Bishop Francis said without enthusiasm. As far as he was concerned, he would have preferred candlelight in front of holy icons.

"How do you know that the track is not damaged and the tunnel is not collapsed somewhere far away and deep underground?" Archbishop Avanella asked as the floor panel under their feet hummed and the cabin lifted over the track.

"I don't," Victor finally admitted. "It comes with the business, and it's impossible to foresee."

Lord save our souls! both bishops thought. Their journey was about to take another unpredictable turn.

LUCAS OPENED his eyes and found himself on a wooden bed with tin bells hanging from the headboard. Above, he saw a Japanese World War II fighter-jet model suspended from the ceiling. On the wall under it was an old pilot helmet and khaki overalls with Japanese Imperial red-and-white emblems on both sleeves. Two samurai swords were also on the wall, one on each side. The bells chimed as he turned to see the rest of the room, which was also filled with WWII relics.

"Ah, so you finally woke up." Thomas entered the room. "How are you? Feeling better?"

"I think so…" Lucas checked his wounded hands and rolled up a sleeve of his robe, revealing traces of torture on his arm.

"It will heal quickly," Thomas said. "It's extrodinary how quickly you recovered after everything you've been through." He turned to someone behind him. "Please, Alex, let me introduce my dear friend." The old professor pointed at Alex. "Lucas, this is the man who saved your life." The young men shook hands.

"Ouch," Lucas said. "It still hurts… I hope you won't be offended if I say the blood of the Messiah saved me first? And you were the second, for which I am infinitely grateful to you."

"Not at all," Alex chuckled. "I will only say that it was the most difficult virtual show in my life."

"Where is Meg?" Lucas said. "Is she safe?"

"She continues your mission. She is trying to find those healed by the Messiah," Thomas said.

"But couldn't she wait for me?"

"You don't belong there. This is the hiding place for women to whom He gave new life, or so they say," Thomas paused. "She asked me to tell you that she loves you and that you should wait for her return."

"This will be very difficult for me," Lucas said. "What else happened while I was out?"

"A lot of things, unfortunately." The professor sighed.

Lucas remained silent for a long time after he heard about the verdict and the pandemic. He got out of bed and walked across the room.

"Do you know where they keep the Messiah?" he said, turning to the professor.

"Area 51," Thomas said. "They set up a donor center there, with only one donor. They will slowly kill him, bleeding him to death. People say there is some local doctor in charge of the procedure."

"I know this doctor," Lucas said quietly, as if talking to himself. "He helped me to survive and betrayed HIM, all at the same time. How's this possible?"

"Torture and fear untie tongues well," Thomas said. "I don't know how I would behave in this situation."

"It's better to never experience it, and if it does happen, it's better to die," Lucas looked up at him. "If only I could see Dr. Portnoy again. I have something to tell him. He'd understand."

"First, we must free the Messiah or whoever they call Messiah," Thomas reminded him. "Frankly, I still have my doubts, but let's leave that for later."

"You still don't trust your heart, Thomas?" Lucas said. "I think it's about time to start following your heart and believing."

"Maybe, but I still need more time." The professor raised his hand, stopping Lucas, who tried to disagree. "Please don't ask how long it might take. Instead let me tell you my plan." He turned to Alex. "All our hopes are on him and his talent."

"I don't know if I can do it." Alex shrugged. "I can't promise. It's one thing to arrange a virtual air show but quite another to open the gates of an impregnable fortress. But, I'll give it a try."

"I know Meg could help," said Lucas. "If only she'd be able to find these women and the resurrected girl."

The roar of a military vehicle's engine outside drowned out Lucas's last words.

"Who is that?"

"I think it's the SS," Alex said. "I didn't expect them so early."

Taken by surprise, they had no time to put up a fight. As armed guards burst into the room, Alex leapt toward a sword on the wall, but one of the soldiers knocked him down with a rifle butt. Two other soldiers grabbed Lucas, and an officer in a brown shirt with SS silver arrows handcuffed the professor's wrists.

"Take them all to the camp, and shoot them if they attempt to escape," said the officer. "And burn this shithole to the ground."

Crimson flames engulfed the farm as the van containing the arrested drove out of the gate. The burning fighter above it crashed to the ground on its final flight.

CHAPTER 51
CAVE OF A THOUSAND FACES

FOLLOWING THE PROFESSOR'S DIRECTIONS, Meg located the former planetarium building, a tall window-less structure with a broken glass door on the ground floor. "COME TO SEE THE FUTURE" read an old poster over the entrance. The area around the building was deserted as most of the residents in this poor neighborhood were ravaged by the pandemic.

Meg made her way inside and, navigating through the shards of glass crunching under her feet, went down to the underground garage. There weren't any signs of people hiding there, just cars. Rows of dead Teslas, Fords, Dodges, and one Ferrari were covered with a thick layer of dust and were untouched. She stood before the red body of the Ferrari. It was the 912 Spider model that she knew well from past happy years. She felt again like a young carefree girl discovering the world. Forgetting about her mission for a moment, she snuck into the Ferrari salon. Drowning in the expensive leather and breathing in the aroma of a long-forgotten life, full of desires and sensations, she could not believe what the world turned into just a few years later—into this darkness of broken dreams and dashed hopes for a happier life. Everything had crashed in the name of greed, conformity, and false security, she thought. Her first desire was to start the engine and, listening to the music of a thousand angry horses, speed away from this nightmare that kept her here.

Meg suddenly noticed a dark figure moving between the cars. Someone was here, alive. Trying not to make any noise, she opened the door and climbed out. She stood still, listening to the footsteps nearby. Someone had stopped and must be listening, too, but then the steps began to recede.

"Hey, who's there?" Meg turned on her flashlight and directed its beam at the stranger. The figure turned around, and Meg saw a frightened female face.

"Don't be afraid, I will not harm you!" Meg said, approaching the stranger.

The woman drew back, attempting to run away, but Meg took her hand. The handkerchief fell from her head and the golden hair fell over her shoulders. She was very young, not more than fifteen.

"I will not harm you," Meg reassured her. "What's your name?"

The girl did not respond, looking at her with blue frightened eyes.

"My name is Meg. What is yours?"

"Kim...Kimberly," the girl finally said.

"Do you live here? Where are the others?"

"They..." The girl paused. "My mom and sisters are here, behind this door. Others are farther down—many of them. You won't betray us? We're hiding from the SS and the police."

"Police no longer exist. But why are you hiding?"

"We all worship one God who healed us and whom evil forces want to kill."

"Are you talking about the Messiah? SS guards have already arrested him and sentenced him to death. We must free him," Meg said. "We have little time left. Take me to the others."

"I can't," the girl said.

"You *must* if you love the One who healed you. This is His only chance." Meg looked into her eyes. "He saved me too, and now I pray for him."

The girl hesitated for a moment and finally made up her mind. She came to the service door at the end of the parking lot and made a silent gesture to follow her.

Kim's family, her mother and two sisters, happily accepted the newcomer. Seeing their bright faces, glowing with kindness, Meg could not believe that one of them was once critically ill and that only a miracle saved her.

"Which of you was healed by the Messiah?" Meg asked.

"Kimberly," the mother said. "She was born deaf and paralyzed. We prayed for her healing for fourteen years."

"Kim?" Meg looked at the smiling girl. "You are a very lucky girl, you know that?" She hugged her new friend.

Together, they went farther into the dungeon after Meg asked them to show her the rest of those who were cured by the Messiah. Going down the endless stairs, they found themselves in a huge karst cave lit by hundreds of bonfires where people were warming themselves.

"A legend says that this was a sacred site for Indian tribes," the mother explained. "According to legend, the axis of the earth and the gods converge here."

"How many people are here?" Meg asked. "And why are they all women?"

"Thousands," the mother said. "It was easier for us to pray separately. We are all praying for the Messiah…"

"Praying may not be enough." Meg looked into the faces around her.

"We must set Him free!" she said loudly, and her words echoed in the cave. "Just as He freed us from our illnesses and delivered us from Evil!"

Hundreds of faces turned to her.

"Wait, aren't you *that* woman? The one the Messiah called Magdalene?" said an elderly woman whose head was wrapped in a black handkerchief. A whisper of hundreds of voices passed through the cave.

"Come and join us—we remember you," the woman said.

CHAPTER 52
THE END

THERE WAS LESS and less blood in Him. The end was approaching. The Condemned no longer raised his head, no longer trying to say anything, no longer asked to have the blindfold removed from his eyes. His arms hung lifeless on the cross and did not flinch when medics pierced them with needles, attaching new tubes to drain the last drops of his blood. Portnoy ordered the removal of the blindfold and was struck to see no trace of reproach in J. C.'s eyes. Tears flowed down His face, tears of joy, as if He saw his bright end. It was unbearable for the doctor to watch this. It would be easier if the tortured man shouted, begged for mercy, or cursed his tormentors. Portnoy realized that he could never bring himself to forget who was in front of him—to forget that he was killing the Messiah with his own hands. *My hands are covered in blood*—His *blood,* he thought.

"Untie him and take him to the vault below," Portnoy said when he saw that the executed man had no chance of survival. "Give him some water, be gentle with him."

"Excuse me, doctor, but the verdict says that the release of blood can only be interrupted by the death of the condemned," said the senior assistant, a man in his forties, sent from the Human Shelter.

"Do as I said and come back here. We will start a new procedure," Portnoy said, removing his lab coat. "I take full responsibility."

Lab assistants put J. C. on a stretcher and carried him down. The staircase leading to the basement ended in front of a huge round door, like those armored doors found in bank vaults. It took several men to open it. Inside the crypt were stone walls dotted with hieroglyphs.

"What are these inscriptions?" one of the assistants wondered.

"Nobody knows," the team leader said. "They were here long before this base was built. Some say it is the room of secret knowledge."

"It's creepy…" the young man muttered.

"Put him here," the team leader said, pointing to the middle of the room. "And, give him some water, although it's probably useless." He checked the dying man's pulse. "I don't think he has much time left. He saved thousands of lives—leave him in peace."

The assistants hurried out of the spine-chilling room, closing the door, thick and heavy as a tombstone.

Goliath drove his Hummer up to the tower when it was getting dark. The guards at the entrance lit torches and escorted the Centurion upstairs. Everything was quiet, too quiet, and Goliath did not like it.

"You must keep an eye on the doctor and his assistants. Why are there no guards inside the tower?" his voice boomed on the stairs.

"All unchanged, sir. Blood is collected in sufficient quantities," said the head guard. "It's surprising how one person can have so much blood."

"We'll see about that." Quickly passing two more flights, Goliath kicked the door open...and froze in place. The doctor's body hung on the cross. It was entangled in tubes; the containers at his feet were full of blood.

"Son of a..." Goliath exclaimed. He checked the body, which was lifeless and getting cold. "He escaped!" The Centurion turned around. "Hey, lab rats—all of you!"

Frightened laboratory assistants gathered in the room.

"He ordered us to do it," said the head assistant. "We were told to use every drop of the doctor's blood instead."

"And, where did the condemned man go? Where are you hiding him?"

"He's in the basement. He's dead too... We...we tried to revive him," the head assistant said, stammering with fear. "W...we were following orders."

"I'll see about that," Goliath said.

Leaving the room, he turned to the head of the guards.

"Give me your rifle, and lock up these rats."

A thunderstorm was gathering in the desert around the base, the wind was picking up, and lightning tore through the night sky as Goliath headed downstairs.

CHAPTER 53
FINDING HOPE

"DID YOU SEE THE RESURRECTED GIRL?" Magdalene kept asking the women, walking from group to group. Finally, one of the females remembered that she had seen the strange girl whom many avoided because of her frightening eyes.

"Yes, her name is Hope," the woman said. "She was here. She was always alone."

"Where can I find her?" Magdalene asked.

"She left." The woman tried to remember.

"She didn't say where she was going?"

"She hardly spoke." The woman shook her head. "Although…wait a minute, yes, she mentioned something. It was difficult to understand, something about how she must see Him."

"Who?"

"I don't know. *Him*, she said."

———

Wandering through the deserted streets, Hope approached the abandoned department store. The family she admired before was still there, behind the only unbroken glass of the display window. This time, she looked closely at the mother —at her slender tanned body in a revealing yellow bikini barely covered by a light beach shirt, oversized plastic bracelets on her arms, and a beach bag, which she held casually, ostensibly preparing to toss it on the warm yellow sand. The woman was graceful and full of life. She seemed about to laugh at Hope's pale face and her awkward figure in the dirty dress. Hope kept standing in front of the beatiful woman, confronting her, then turned, picked up a piece of asphalt from the sidewalk and smashed the window. Shards fell to the ground with a crash that could be heard throughout the city. Hope slowly stepped from the street into the shop window and disappeared into the department store.

After a short time, she returned to the street transformed, now wearing a white cloak, high heels, brand-name sunglasses, and a layer of makeup that hid the pallor of her face. In her hands, she held a beach bag. Rare passersby moved aside when they saw her on the street. They were just as frightened by the defiantly attractive woman among the city ruins as they were seeing the walking dead.

"Honey, you're five years late," said one, plucking up courage. "They don't wear that now. For such a daring look, you can be sent to hard labor these days or a death camp if you have a record."

She continued on her way, left the city, and stopped the first military truck. It was loaded with empty blood containers.

"Where to?" said the young driver, ogling the attractively dressed woman. "Straight to jail, or do you want to warm up first?" Confident that his uniform would shield him from a soliciting charge, he figured it was fine to have some "fun."

She threw open her coat, revealing her body in the yellow bikini.

"I'll be damned!" The soldier's eyes flashed. "You're a damn cool chick."

He let her in.

"Let me see you closer." He put both hands on her. "Gee, you're ice-cold, but that's fine, I'll warm you up." His hands reached her bra, and he began breathing faster. "Yeah, that's nice, let's see what we got inside…"

She moved closer, leaning against him, and as he tried to kiss her, she reached for the door handle on his side and pushed him out of the truck with unexpected force.

The truck sped away with a new driver.

"I'll kill you, bitch!" the shocked soldier shouted after her.

It was noon, and the sun-baked desert steamed after the overnight thunderstorm. Splashing through puddles, the truck quickly reached Area 51. It passed the dilapidated hangars on the airfield and the abandoned fleet of service vehicles and drove up to the checkpoint in front of the Tower. An SS guard leaned out of the booth and was dumbfounded when he saw Hope behind the wheel.

"Halt!" He came to the truck. "Get out!" The guard pointed his Kalashnikov at her. His astonishment grew even more when he saw her, almost naked, standing in front of him.

"You must be expensive," he said, forgetting to ask where the real driver was.

"How much do you charge?" The guard gave Hope an appraising look.

"Hey, what's going on here?" said another guard who approached them.

"Look what we got," the first guard said. "A hooker, straight from the big city. The boss has left. We can have some fun here!"

Wasting no time, the guards grabbed the teenage girl and carried her inside the Tower.

CHAPTER 54

FINAL DESTINATION

"WELL, what should I do with you?" an SS investigator said when the arrested were taken from the farm to the concentration camp.

In Lucas's eyes, the officer was too young to be taken seriously, so he decided to test him.

"What do you accuse us of?" he said. "Why did you detain us?"

"Here, I ask questions, not you," the officer stated. Although he pretended to be harsh, the very fact that he reacted to Lucas's question showed his inexperience.

Any other time, I would be beaten to a pulp, Lucas thought. *It's a good sign.*

"Take a look here." The investigator showed Lucas the mug shot taken during his first arrest. "And here…" The investigator unfolded a poster for Alex's Pearl Harbor show featuring an attacking Japanese bomber.

"The same bomber attacked us three days before," the officer said. "And now, the most important thing…" He came to Lucas and opened Lucas's shirt, revealing the fresh wound.

"This is the mark of our quality control. It means you were dead, but you are sitting here in front of me, alive, and you have antibodies in your blood, though you have not been vaccinated. How do you explain this?"

Lucas realized that he was in a hopeless position, and this time, no help was coming.

"Speak fast, I have little time," the officer suggested.

"I need to talk to your superior. I have very important information," Lucas said, trying to buy some time.

"You asked for it," the officer grinned. "In a few minutes, the First Centurion will be here and you will be finished, this time once and for all!"

Goliath arrived at the concentration camp in a depressed mood. In his mind's eye was a lifeless body on a round stone in the middle of the underground room. He pierced it with a bayonet to properly do his job. As soon as the metal entered the chest between the fifth and sixth ribs, a storm of visions fell upon the Centurion: his childhood in a small town where everyone marveled at his enormous strength; the first murder, which he committed accidentally when he was seventeen; his poverty growing up; and fights, countless fights from which he always emerged victorious. His main feeling was hatred— disgust for everything and everyone that surrounded him, especially pathetic, miserable people who he enjoyed killing. His service in the SS forces provided an outlet for the hatred that gripped him.

Upon learning of the detainees, Centurion ordered them to be taken to the execution chamber, a large room with dirty cement walls in the basement of the former airport. He had neither the time nor the inclination to conduct a thorough investigation. Bending under the law ceiling, he entered the cell, unbuttoning his pistol holster. All three detainees were lying face down on the floor, their hands handcuffed behind their backs. Goliath turned the prisoners over one by one, peering into their faces.

"Who will be the first? Who am I going to kill?" he asked, expecting to see fear in their eyes.

The arrested were silent. Finally, Lucas said, "You can start with me, but only after I reveal one secret."

The centurion was surprised. "Is it you who managed to escape from here? I saw your picture." His eyes settled on the young man. "Who put on this freak air attack show? One of those two or both?" He pointed to Alex and Thomas.

"No, I did it myself. What I'll tell you now will help save thousands of more lives."

"Do you think I'm interested?" Goliath smirked. "Well then, speak!"

"Only after you let my friends go."

The Centurion was taken aback by such impudence. This little man, who was in his hands and with whom he can do anything, dared to bargain! What was it, simple stupidity, shock or was he out of his mind? The improbability of the situation was beginning to amuse the Centurion.

"You know who I am? How many people have I disposed of with my bare hands?" he said. "I will kill you quickly so you don't suffer much! How about that for a bargain?"

Silence followed his "offer."

At the next moment, an underground rumble echoed throughout the building. Then the chamber walls began to shake more and more.

"It must be an earthquake!" the investigator, who stood behind Goliah said, looking around fearfully. "We must leave."

"Run, you coward, but I must finish them off first before they get away." The Centurion still wanted to enjoy the bloody show, which he was about to put on. He raised his pistol, but just then, the wall collapsed, raising dense clouds of dust, and a huge steel cylinder was pushed inside.

"What the…" the Centurion said, pointing his weapon at the strange object. "Guards!"

The soldiers, who were about to flee but were afraid of their commander, carefully made their way through the rubble into the room.

"Check who is inside," said the Centurion. He was unfamiliar with the feeling of fear, as well as most other human emotions. "And, find those arrested under the rubble, so they won't escape."

Lucas rose to his feet, holding his cuffed hands behind his back. The soldiers pulled out the others. Thomas was barely breathing, and Alex was bleeding from a head wound.

"Check if everyone is here," Goliath said, turning his attention to the mysterious cylinder. "What is this, a new trick to help you escape?" he asked Lucas. "Who set it up?"

Lucas was surprised too. They all watched as the steel door opened and Victor, sweaty and confused, appeared in front of them.

"Are… we in hell?" he asked.

"You?" Lucas said. "Could you find a worse time?"

CHAPTER 55

AWAITING EXECUTION

"NOW I UNDERSTAND," said Lucas. "The execution chamber is the deepest section of the airport subsurface level, where they planned to build tunnels for electric cars under the entire city to ease traffic jams. No wonder you ended up here."

"Pure coincidence," said Victor. "I had no idea where the central gravity tube ends. We didn't manage to slow down sufficiently to stop in time and we broke through the wall." He fell silent, then looked at his friend. "Sorry, we came to help."

"We see it, great help," Thomas grumbled.

They all sat together, arrested and awaiting execution.

"Strange, why does it take so long? Before, we would've been shot a long time ago," Lucas said, listening to what was happening outside the door of their cell – there was dead silence.

"It's very depressing, thank you," Victor replied sadly. "I was counting on a happier ending though."

"I'm so glad to see you all, though anywhere but here." Lucas eyed his friends. "It's so painful to think that in a way I've killed you."

"Ah, never mind, it happens." Victor was still trying to

carry on their usual joking conversation, but his somber eyes betrayed him. "It's like a bad dream," he added.

"Soon, it will be over. No more dreams, good or bad," said Inspector Frescatto.

"But how did it happen that we came here? What a coincidence!" Victor said after a long pause.

"I don't believe in coincidences," Frescatto said. "I discovered for myself long ago that there is always something behind every chance occurrence, every coincidence."

"You are right, inspector," said Archbishop Avanella. "Only this is not something but *Someone* who directs all of our steps and decisions if our eyes and hearts are open."

"Do you think this is...our Lord?" Bishop Francis asked. "If he brought us into this place, I hope he leads us out of here...alive."

"He will," Avanella said firmly.

Goliath was still in doubt over what to do with the prisoners who fell into his hands. Execute them on the spot as an immediate threat to public safety or complete the investigation of recent events to find out who was behind these attacks? Time was short, and he chose the former. All that remained was to assemble a firing squad, but an unexpected complication arose. Looking into the faces of his soldiers, the Centurion discovered a change—the absence of hatred in their eyes, the most important element that drove the entire SS movement forward. Goliath suddenly felt the earth was slipping from under his feet, and, as he closed his eyes, the cursed vision returned to him involving the body he pierced with the bayonet – *He rises...He comes to him and stares right into the Centurion's heart as if He wants to take it out of his chest. The dead prisoner reaches out to touch him...*

Shuddering, Goliath opened his eyes, shaking off the

vision. He needed to hurry, he headed towards the cell where the prisoners were held, but the head jailer stopped him.

"Centurion, the enemy is approaching. It's the entire army!"

"It's impossible," Goliath waved him off. "All enemies are destroyed except for this handful of detainees, and I'll take care of them myself." He took the officer's machine gun. "Order the guards to shoot to kill. We're not taking prisoners."

"Yes sir, but I'm afraid we no longer have guards. They all…" The officer fell silent.

"What? Speak up!"

"They laid down their arms."

"What?!"

The officer nodded in silence; he was trembling all over. "I can't do anything. Please court-martial me…"

"That would be too good for you," Goliath said, his face turning crimson. "I'll kill you in front of your soldiers—maybe then, they'll be ready to fight."

"Do what you want, Centurion. I…I don't understand what's going on." The old seasoned jailer stood before him, pitiful and helpless.

"Then I'll shoot you right now." Still holding the officer's Kalashnikov in his left hand, Goliath pulled out a pistol and shot at the jailer's confused face. The old man began to sink to the floor.

"One is done, others are still to go…" the Centurion muttered, heading to the exit. Soon, more shots rang out in the passages of the concentration camp.

CHAPTER 56
ESCAPING DEATH

PEOPLE FLOCKED ALONG ALL the roads leading to the airport. Thousands of women in black clothes and local residents joined them. This was a sea of enlightened faces. Magdalene walked in front, ready to face death. The camp gates were open; no guards were there except for a few soldiers lying lifeless on the ground. Inside, they found more bodies. This was the trail of the Centurion.

Magdalene rushed through the premises, checking the dead and fearing she would see Lucas. He was not among them. Suddenly, a powerful grenade went off somewhere in the depths of the building. Everyone headed toward the roar of the explosion. They found the underground chamber devastated by the blast, the walls pierced by shrapnel, and part of the ceiling collapsed, but all of the prisoners were alive, albeit shell-shocked.

"Luke!" Magdalene ran to him.

The women began to take apart the wreckage, freeing other captives.

"Meg?" he said.

"Magdalene." She smiled happily. "I found my true name as well as yours."

"Darling…" he whispered.

"I don't follow. How come they changed their names?" Thomas asked, brushing off the dust. "And how did we survive the explosion? The Centurion threw the grenade right between us!"

"This is a sign," said archbishop Avanella, who had joined them. "And, who are you, my child?" He turned to Magdalene. "And who are these women who follow you?"

"We are all servants of God, healed by Him from mental and physical wounds," she said.

"You found them," Luke said with relief, "as we hoped. My mind still refuses to accept that I'm alive. We all had to die, and there was no way out. It's like walking through a gallery of the rooms of your life. You pass one, you face the wall, and it seems that this is the end, but suddenly the door opens and you see the next room, and the next until you finally confront Death. But he recedes, never going away though as if luring you into a trap…"

"Don't strain yourself." Magdalene wiped the blood from his forehead. "Someday, we will understand everything."

"Avanella, everybody, we mustn't waste time. We must free Him," Bishop Francis said. "Who will lead us?"

Alex stepped forward. "I will show you the way. I know the area."

"We will follow you then," archbishop Avanella said, looking around at the crowd. "Everyone who is still capable, follow us!"

On the other side of the airport, Goliath stepped out of the service exit. His uniform was torn and his hands covered in blood. The Centurion knew who was to blame for his failure. He was still alive and had to die now, once and for all.

CHAPTER 57
THE LIGHT

THEY LEFT THE CITY, an army of thousands: women, men, and children. More and more soldiers joined them, too, dropping their weapons.

"This is our army that everyone was expecting," said archbishop Avanella.

"I would've preferred the soldiers had kept their weapons though," bishop Francis remarked. "We may still need them. But why this change of heart? Why did they join us? These soldiers were ruthless robots, programmed to kill, to obey most brutal commands and suddenly such a radical transformation. Just look at their faces – they are people again with human feelings and emotions."

"It's a mystery to me too," Thomas said. "They were about to kill us. That's what they've been doing."

"This is my secret, which I offered to reveal in exchange for your freedom," Luke said.

"I don't follow." The old professor looked at him questioningly.

"*His* blood not only heals disease but also changes people, makes them better. None of them will follow criminal orders anymore. They will pass on this part of God to others. The pandemic will end."

"I hope you're right," the professor said. "So far, it's working well."

"Walking on foot is too slow—we may be too late to save Him," bishop Francis said. "We need wheels, something to get there fast." He looked around and pointed to an airport service van abandoned by the road. "Like this bus, though this one is probably broken."

"Of course it broke down, otherwise no one would've left it," Thomas said.

"Let me check what I can do about it," Victor suggested.

"Me too." Alex joined him.

They approached the old Ford Transit, which had long since exhausted its working life, and opened the engine.

———

Goliath left the service van halfway to Area 51. The engine stalled, and there was no time to find out what was wrong with it. Making huge strides, the Centurion marched toward the base. The shlagbaum on the road in front of it was raised, and no guards could be seen. Approaching the Tower, he saw the military AM General truck and, on the ground, a woman's bright summer raincoat stained by the prints of soldier's boots. The gate leading inside was thrown open. Goliath grabbed his dagger and entered the Tower. It was time to confront his enemy. His vision had changed so that he could no longer see any colors, only gray tones, darker and lighter. The same thing happened with his feelings. They flowed out, like water flows out of a damaged vessel, leaving only a cold empty space. Again and again, he saw His motionless body, as if hanging in the air, which he needed to deprive of the last remnants of life. Something, some energy or unknown force continued to live in Him despite the mortal wounds. He must stop it.

To accomplish his mission, Goliath had the *tecpatl*, an

ancient dagger that Aztec priests used during human sacri-fices. His goal was to cut out the heart of his enemy, the One, who by his very existence threatened the New Order. Jumping over the steps, the Centurion quickly went down to the basement, opened the multi-ton door with one jerk—and froze in a stream of light emanating from the chamber. It was so intense that it stopped the giant, forcing him to kneel. *What is the matter with me?* thought the Centurion. *I must not give in, I must do my duty!*

CHAPTER 58

ASCENSION

THE REVIVED Ford Transit held twelve people—the bishops, Luke, Magdalene, Victor, and the core members of the crew. They all drove to Area 51. The shlagbaum on the road in front of the base was raised, and no guards could be seen. Approaching the Tower, they saw the military truck and a woman's raincoat on the ground revealing the prints of soldiers' boots. The gate leading inside was wide open.

They stepped into the Tower. There were no guards inside. Avanella paused at the stairs, not knowing where to go, and they all walked towards the ghostly radiance that rose from the dungeon. The gentle light intensified as they came to the entrance of the chamber. The corners of the room were drowning in darkness. In the middle, on a low pedestal, lay the Shroud covering the body of the deceased. An inexplicably quiet but penetrating light came from it. This light illuminated Hope's ghostly face, smeared with lipstick and dripping mascara. Wearing a rough gray tunic, she kneeled at the foot of the pedestal.

"Who is it?" Avanella asked in a whisper to his teammates.

"The One who saved the Relic," Thomas said, pointing at the Shroud.

The body under the Shroud gradually shrunk until the cloth lay empty on the pedestal. Hope's sobs became louder and were answered with heavy sighs in the corner of the room. Everyone looked there and turned numb, seeing the huge back and bowed head of the former Centurion. Tears of remorse ran down the giant's face.

"Wonderful are thy works, O Lord," Avanella said.

"Now that I see it with my own eyes, I believe it," Thomas said quietly. "I never thought this moment would ever come."

They all watched as Hope got up and walked to the wall. Dipping fingers into her eyes like an inkwell, she wrote:

DESCENSUS CHRISTI AD INFEROS

CHAPTER 59

CONDEMNED

"WHAT?" archbishop Avanella froze in horror. Behind him, Francis choked, gasping for air. The others waited, puzzled by the despair written on the bishops' faces.

Strong and confident just a moment before, Avanella suddenly changed, turning into a person who had suffered an unexpected disaster.

He looked around helplessly as if seeing everything for the first time. "No!!" He shook his head in desperation and fell to his knees.

"It says we are not alive," bishop Francis stammered. "We... all of us... are dead!"

Cold waves passed through the chamber. Everyone stared at the inscription in mute fear—and it looked back at them, standing out in black letters among other mysterious messages:

DESCENSUS CHRISTI AD INFEROS –

DESCENT OF CHRIST TO HELL

Life flashed before their eyes, stopping at an almost imperceptible moment—the moment that brought each of them into this crypt…

———

Magdalene shuddered. She found herself far away in the ocean. The weather changed, and the waves grew angry when she turned back to the shore. They attacked her, smashing her face, blinding her, and pushing her underwater with increasing force. She was a good swimmer and struggled against the current with the confidence of a former champion, not realizing the danger. But then it became clear to her that she might lose the battle. In short pauses between furious blows to her face, she saw the bubbling outline of the Santa Lucia Mountains. The shoreline was still far away—too far. All she could do now was to keep diving under rising waves, holding her breath and imagining she was a mermaid, her favorite fairy tale character as a child. At one point, she missed the ocean's rhythm and came to the surface too early, only to be struck by a heavy, concrete-like wave. The murky world embraced her and pulled her down into its silent depths. She felt as the blood was coming out of her mouth; the ocean wiped it from her face, pulling her deeper and deeper. It would have been so easy to stop fighting and give in. She was falling through the curtains of the dark world that opened in front of her, vaguely recording in her dying mind that she had begun to inhale water in sporadic shallow gasps. She no longer strived to go back. *Time stood still in the damp, oppressive silence, covering her like a tombstone.*

———

Victor suddenly trembled all over, as if awakening in a new eerie reality. He remembered an article in the *New Amsterdam Times*, which he initially took for a practical joke. It read:

> *"Police found a body on a sidewalk in front of a building in Lower Manhattan. According to police sources, the CEO of Big Apple Solutions, Victor Adams, 29, was the victim of a burglary gone wrong. Criminals broke into the victim's four-story luxury apartment, seizing electronics and other valuable items as Mr. Adams returned home."*

…several strangers in black hoodies were rummaging in his things when he returned from a short walk to a pier on the East River. Neither they nor he expected to see each other.

"Shi-i-it," said their leader. "This cheeky fella's back. Hey, Pooch, take care of him."

Somebody's hand grabbed Victor by the throat and pulled to the window. Gasping for breath, he saw how a window frame, that hasn't been open for years, went up and cold wind burst into the room… the city with shiny skyscrapers, green parks, rushing cars and lights opened before him – it was bright and incredibly beautiful… that's how he remembered it… forever…

> *"According to the police report, the victim was thrown out of a rooftop window and fell to his death."*

———

Archbishop Avanella and his team were once again in distress in the middle of the Atlantic on the yacht. The hours stretched out into infinity. The tempest pounded Santa *Maria* from all directions. Gusts of wind bent the masts, and jets of rain flooded the cockpit windows. The waves grew in size, reaching toward the sky—and then, illuminated by lightning strikes, a black wall of water rose in front of the yacht and brought down its thousand-ton weight on them...It plunged the *Santa Maria* into the abyss of water, only to grab it the next moment and throw it into the sky. She froze in the air, hanging for long seconds, turned upside down, and began to slide back into the ocean.

That's it, the yacht capsized, it's over, he thought. *We're falling into a watery grave. To you I cry from the depths, O Lord, have mercy on our souls!*

––––––

Luke saw himself again in the burning cathedral. The nave of the cathedral was filled with dense smoke, so he put his gas mask on. The beam of his flashlight snatched from the darkness parts of marble pillars, rows of oak seats, and the main aisle leading to the basilica. It would be impossible to save the cathedral if flames reached this part of the building. He ran down the aisle into the depths of the building as something huge and heavy collapsed on top of him... When he opened his eyes, he saw his own lifeless body, lying on the floor next to a smoldering roof rafter. He was not breathing, and the last words of his father in the *capella* suddenly reached him: *Welcome home son. I was waiting for you. We saved Him... you and I...*

But what do you call home, papa? It is dark, scary and miserable here, he asked.

Home is where we're destined to be, said his father, *and his face lit up in the darkness, like the light of a midnight church candle... Descensus Christi ad Inferos...*

"We are all damned, and we are all in hell," Luke muttered in despair. He looked at his friends, crushed by what they had just learned, their faces a whiter shade of pale.

FINAL CHAPTER
ACCORDING TO LUKE

We found the crypt to be dark and cold once again. We stood there yarning to understand what had taken place before us. To what had we borne witness? Great fear crept into our souls, and I asked my fellow journeyers how we crossed the line between life and death without seeing? How did it come to pass that we died at different times? Yet we stand here still, in this dungeon, before the place from which our Savior ascended into heaven.

Whereupon the archbishop declared unto us, 'time is no more in the Afterworld.'

For what sins, my companions asked, have we been rendered unto this place?

To which the archbishop replied, it is your daily transgressions that have sealed your fate.

Alas, I declared, where was the devil, how is it that we do not see him?

The devil, the teacher proclaimed, was in our corrupt souls. And as he said this, we saw the great darkness around us thickening. To what hope can we cling, I asked.

The archbishop pointed at the resurrected girl whose name meant hope. Our only hope for salvation, he said, is in our truest feelings, now and forever, amen.

EPILOGUE

NO ONE REMEMBERED how long they stood shell-shocked, trying to grasp what had happened to them—to the entire world around, which suddenly lost all of its colors and now appeared in its true light, passing through them like deathly x-rays.

"How did it happen that we crossed the line between life and death without noticing it?" Luke finally said. "And at different times? Some earlier, some later, and yet we see each other, we speak. How come we didn't know we were dead?"

"Time is irrelevant in the Afterworld." Avanella slowly raised his head. His recent confusion passed and his face brightened.

"But why are we here? For what sins?"

"Well, if only it were as simple as the Church sometimes tries to present it to us. Apparently, we somehow dug our graves without even noticing it."

"But where was the devil?" Lucas suddenly asked. "He wasn't among any murderers, so why don't we see him?"

"Hasn't it become clear to you just yet?" Avanella said. "The real evil is in all of us... The question is how deep it has gotten inside. And it is far more dangerous than any monster attacking us!"

The darkness around them thickened, and they felt that they were slowly, inevitably falling into some huge black hole...deeper and deeper...or was it HE, who ascended in front of them through the dungeon vaults, leaving them in gaping depths filled with groans and pain? The ONE who was their link to insurmountable heights, the ONE who they awaited so long and nearly failed to recognize when HE appeared among them? Or was HE merely a dream, just a dream, like their existence?

"Can we still keep hope?"

"Maybe. Look at the girl." The archbishop pointed to the teenager bent over against the wall under the ominous inscription she had just written. "Her very name indicates hope. She is dead, and her only document is her death certificate, but she made it possible for Him to escape from hell where he was delivered by us humans. There are three unaccounted days when He lay in the tomb before resurrection. His Spirit visited us fallen spirits. 'He went and proclaimed to the spirits in prison because they formerly did not obey.' That's from Peter 3:18."

Luke stared at the inscription.

"But it was much longer than three days that He was here." He eyed Avanella. "And He resurrected in two days from Friday's burial to Sunday, not three days. How is this all possible?"

"All I can say is that our human time is apparently irrelevant in the Afterworld; it can move in all directions." Avanella put his hand on Luke's shoulder and smiled, trying to cheer up his comrade. "Our true feelings, that's what counts now and forever."

Luke's head was swimming. He could not stop asking his friend questions just to keep his mind away from the horrible reality that was crushing them all. "But then, why did He save us from the killer virus? And, did He really save us if we are already dead?"

"According to the ancient scriptures, there are many layers in the Afterworld. He helped us stay here so that we would not fall even further into the 'fiery hyena.' "

"But, is there any way out? How do we get out of here?"

The archbishop pondered. He, too, had tried to find the answer to this question. "All we can do is pray," he said finally. "Maybe, just maybe, we will find the way." He eyed the young man. "And you, what will you do now when your mission is over?"

Luke fell silent. He stared at his friends and studied the mysterious inscriptions on the crypt's walls. "*Over*, you say? Not really." He approached the dais with the Shroud on it and quietly lifted the veil. He gently ran his hand over the surface of the stone on which the body of the Messiah lay, and with trepidation began to fold the still-luminous fabric. "I will bring it back to Turin."

"What about her?" The archbishop pointed to Magdalene, who was praying with the rest of the group. "Will you be able to forget your feelings?"

"Never, and I hope she feels the same and she follows me," Luke said. "We still need to rebuild the cathedral…and our love."

"How sweet!" said Savorelli, wedging himself into the conversation. "Don't forget the food. You'd all starve to death without me! I am going with you."

"Inspector," Luke turned to Frescatto. "Please take it." He passed the Shroud to his friend. "You successfully completed the investigation, for which you paid with your life. You deserve the right to deliver it to the people of Turin as an officer of the law."

"You are too generous, my friend," the inspector was a little confused, accepting the honor. "Now, we can all sail back across the ocean without fear."

Raising his hands, Avanella blessed the people so dear to

him. "You're right, my friends. Together, we have nothing to fear!"

"Will you navigate us back home?" The archbishop addressed bishop Francis and was surprised at his hesitant appearance.

"Friends, I think you already have an experienced pilot," Bishop Francis turned to his followers. "Who will take you safely to your home harbor. The archbishop has learned everything I know, including sea navigation, while I... I will stay here."

"Forgive me, my dear friend." He eyed Avanella. "This devastated city is in desperate need of help, and I will do everything in my power to heal its wounds."

"Of course," Avanella hugged his friend. "We'll miss you dearly though."

Luke came to Avanella, took his hand and touched the ring on the archbishop's finger with his lips. "I will write about this, about everything that I have witnessed," he said, "to preserve it forever like this interplanetary graffiti on the walls."

"You must, Luke. You must," Avanella said. "And, I will pray for it."

THE END

ACKNOWLEDGMENTS

I express utmost gratitude to my friend and editor, Stephanie Larkin, for her belief in this project; Kieran Larkin for his expertise and valuable insights; my editor, Katherine Abraham; my daughter, Katherine, and her husband, Aaryn Anderson, for PR, book cover design, and a variety of other responsibilities; my family; and, finally, my California friends, Bob Cooper and Dave Rhody, who provided vital editorial and theological support.

ABOUT THE AUTHOR

An author of several books published in both the US and Europe, Alexander Suslov has been a writer/producer for major radio and TV networks and received a Ph.D. degree from Georgetown University. He lives in the US and France and is currently at work on the second part of DEAD SOULS AWAKENING.